T0332999

Moonlight

Guy de Maupassant

Moonlight

Translated by
Siân Miles

PENGUIN CLASSICS
an imprint of
PENGUIN BOOKS

PENGUIN CLASSICS

UK | USA | Canada | Ireland | Australia
India | New Zealand | South Africa

Penguin Books is part of the Penguin Random House group of companies
whose addresses can be found at global.penguinrandomhouse.com.

This selection taken from *A Parisian Affair and Other Stories*, Penguin Classics 2004
This selection published in Little Clothbound Classics 2023
001

Translation copyright © Siân Miles, 2004

Cover design and illustration by Coralie Bickford-Smith

Set in 9.5/13pt Baskerville 10 Pro
Typeset by Jouve (UK), Milton Keynes
Printed and bound in Great Britain by Clays Ltd, Elcograf S.p.A.

The authorized representative in the EEA is Penguin Random House Ireland,
Morrison Chambers, 32 Nassau Street, Dublin DO2 YH68

A CIP catalogue record for this book is available from the British Library

ISBN: 978-0-241-61980-3

Contents

Moonlight

The abbé Marignan lived up to his illustrious name. His unwavering faith was as solid as a rock and he believed he understood God, as well as his every wish, intention and design. As he walked on the path leading to his little country presbytery he would sometimes ask himself why God had done a certain thing. He would think very carefully, and after putting himself in God's position he nearly always discovered a reason. Far be it from him to murmur in a moment of pious humility, 'O Lord, how mysterious are thy ways . . .' Instead, he would say, 'I am God's servant on earth. Therefore it is right that I should know the reason for his actions and, if I don't, to hazard a pretty good guess what it might be.'

Everything in nature seemed to him to have been created with impeccable and admirable logic. Every great 'Why?' could always be answered by some great 'Because'. Dawns were made so that the world should be glad to rise; daylight so that the crops should ripen; rain for irrigation; evening to prepare for sleep and dark night for slumber itself.

The four seasons similarly met all the needs of agriculture, and never would it have occurred to the priest that nature might have no purpose or that all life might be the product of blind temporal, geographical and physical necessity.

Women, however, were another matter altogether. He loathed them. It was an unconscious loathing based on instinctive mistrust. Often he would quote the words of Christ: 'Woman, what have I to do with thee?' adding, 'It's as if God himself were not happy with that particular work of his.' Woman for him was most certainly the 'twelve times impure' of whom the poet speaks. She was the temptress who had first led man astray and continued to this day her execrable work. She was a weak, dangerous and mysteriously disturbing creature. Even more than her fatal body, he hated her loving soul.

Often he had felt a certain tenderness directed towards himself by women and, though impervious to it, he was irritated by the constant need for love which throbbed within them. In his view God had created woman solely in order to tempt man and thereby to test him. She was to be approached with infinite caution and wariness, as a snare. With her parted lips and arms outstretched towards man she was in fact exactly like a trap. The only exception he made was in the case of nuns, whose vows made them harmless. However, he was sometimes harsh towards even them, sensing within their captive and contrite hearts that same eternal tenderness which, priest or not, got under his skin. He sensed it in their gaze, more tearful and pious than that of monks; he sensed it in the ecstasy which, in their case of course, was mixed up with sex; their surges of love for Christ infuriated him for being, when all was said and done, purely carnal and female. He could feel this wretched tenderness in their docility, in the gentleness of their voices when they addressed him, in their lowered eyes, in their mournful resignation to his rough reprimands. At the door of the convent when he left, he shook out the skirts of his cassock and lengthened his stride as if fleeing from some danger.

Despite all this, he was determined that his niece, who lived with her mother in a little house nearby, should become a nun. She was a pretty, fun-loving young scatterbrain. Whenever the priest pontificated to her she laughed in his face, and when he was cross she hugged him tight and showered him with kisses. He would automatically try to extricate himself from this embrace which, he had to admit, he found absolutely delightful, awakening within him as it did the paternal instinct lying dormant in every living man.

Often as he walked beside her on the meadow paths he would speak to her of God. She scarcely listened and the joy with which she contemplated instead the sky, the grass, and the flowers was reflected in her eyes. Sometimes she would rush off to try and catch some winged creature, crying as she brought it back, 'Look, uncle! Isn't it sweet. Don't you want to give it a little kiss?' This need of hers to kiss butterflies and lilac buds made the priest sick. He was both worried and irritated to find even in her that ineradicable tenderness that lurked always in the heart of woman.

Then one day his sacristan's wife, who did the Abbé Marignan's housework, informed him, choosing her words very carefully, that his niece had a lover. He was appalled when he heard this news as he was shaving, and stood there speechless, with lather all over his face. When he had gathered his wits and could put his thoughts into words again he spluttered: 'It's not true! You're making it up, Mélanie!'

But the simple woman put her hand on her heart.

'As God is my witness, Father, as soon as your sister's gone to bed, off she goes. Along the river they meet. See for yourself between ten and midnight.'

He stopped scratching his chin and, as was his wont when he wanted to think something through, started pacing briskly up and down. Taking up his razor again later, he managed to cut himself three times between the nose and the ear. All day long he remained silent, suppressing his growing anger and indignation. As a priest he was furious at losing a future nun to earthly love. As her moral tutor also he was exasperated. He was like a father to her, after all, the guardian of her soul. And to think that he had been deceived, tricked and cheated by this slip of a girl! He felt all the selfish shock of parents confronted with the news that their daughter has chosen her own husband without or despite their advice.

After dinner he tried to read for a while but failed. His exasperation increased. When the clock struck ten he took up his stick, a formidable oak staff which he always took with him on night visits to the sick. He smiled down at the great cudgel he now twirled menacingly in his horny hand. Suddenly he raised it and, gnashing his teeth as he did so, brought it down on a chair with such force that the back split and it crashed to the floor.

He opened his door and was about to leave when suddenly he stopped in amazement on the threshold of the house. He had rarely in his life seen such magnificent moonlight as now. Like some of the early Christian Fathers, he was blessed with a soul open to rapture and with a poetic disposition. He was suddenly moved, not to say overwhelmed, by the great serenity and beauty of the pale night before him. In his little garden bathed in soft light his rows of fruit trees threw in shadow the shapes of their branches barely in bud; the breath of the huge honeysuckle spreading over the wall of the house wafted its sweet perfume like the soul of fragrance upon the clear and balmy air. He began to breathe deeply himself, drinking it in greedily and slowing down his pace. He was entranced by the scene, so lost in wonder that the thought of his niece all but faded away.

As soon as he reached the open country he stopped in order to contemplate the whole plain which was suffused with this caressing glow and basking serenely in the tender, languid charm of the night. The brief, metallic croak of frogs filled the air on which the notes of a distant nightingale fell one by one. Its clear and delicate song was made more for reverie than reflection and its music to accompany kisses in the magic of the moonlight. As the priest took up his walk again he felt something within him, he knew not what, begin to falter. He felt suddenly tired and weak. He needed to sit down and look, to admire the work of God.

In the distance a long line of poplars snaked along the winding river's edge. A fine, vaporous white mist through which gleaming silver moonbeams shone hovered over and around the banks and enveloped in a transparent cocoon every twist and turn of the waters.

The priest stopped once more, touched to the depths of his soul as he felt growing within him a mounting and irresistible tenderness. He could feel a worrying doubt creep into his thoughts: a question was beginning to grow once more in his mind. Why had God created this? Since night was obviously made for sleep and unconsciousness, rest and all-embracing oblivion, why make it even more lovely than the day and sweeter than any twilight or dawn? Why did this slow and stately star, more beautiful than the sun itself, banish all shadow and illumine things too delicate and mysterious for the light of day? Why did the finest of nature's songbirds not rest like her fellows but sing alone in the darkness of night? Why this veil cast over the world? Why the wild beating of his heart? This yearning of his soul? Why this languor of the body? Why this panoply of loveliness which no one sees if asleep in bed? For whom was this sublime spectacle created, this poetry beamed down from heaven to earth?

The priest could find no answer.

Suddenly in the distance at the meadow's edge, under the arch of trees resplendent in the glistening haze, two shadowy figures walking side by side came into view. The man, the taller of the two, had his arm around the shoulders of his partner and from time to time, drawing her closer to him, he kissed her forehead. The couple gave life to this still landscape which surrounded them like some divine frame. They seemed as one, the single being for whom this calm and silent night was made. They came towards the priest as a living response sent to him by his Maker.

As he stood there stunned and with his heart pounding, the sight before him seemed almost Biblical, like the love of Ruth and Boaz, an expression of God's will set in one of the great scenes of holy writ. Words from the 'Song of Songs' began to form in his mind and the cries of passion, the yearning of the flesh, the fierce, burning ardour of that most tender of poems returned to him.

And he said to himself, 'Perhaps God has created this sort of night in order to imbue the love of man with something of the ideal.' He retreated as the two, entwined, approached ever closer. And though she was his niece he now wondered whether he could disobey the will of God. How could God disapprove of love since he surrounded it with such obvious splendour? Distraught and almost ashamed, he disappeared quickly from sight, as if trespassing in a temple where he had no right to be.

Cockcrow

Madame Berthe d'Avancelles had rejected the advances of her admirer Baron Joseph de Croissard to such an extent that he was now in despair. He had pursued her relentlessly throughout the winter in Paris, and now at his château at Carville in Normandy he was holding a series of hunting parties in her honour.

The husband, Monsieur d'Avancelles, turned a blind eye to all this. It was rumoured that they lived separate lives on account of a physical shortcoming of his which Madame could not overlook. He was a fat little man with short arms, short legs, a short neck, short nose, short everything in fact.

Madame d'Avancelles, in contrast, was a tall, chestnut-haired, determined-looking young woman. She laughed openly at old Pipe and Slippers as she called him to his face but looked with tender indulgence on her admirer, the titled Baron Joseph de Croissard, with his broad shoulders, his sturdy neck and his fair, drooping moustache.

Until now, however, she had granted him no favours despite the fact that he was spending a fortune on her, throwing a constant round of receptions, hunting parties, and all kinds of celebrations to which he invited the local aristocracy.

All day long the woods rang to the sound of hounds in full cry after a fox or a wild boar and every night a dazzling display of fireworks spiralled upwards to join the sparkling stars. A tracery of light from the drawing-room windows shone on the huge lawns where shadowy figures occasionally passed.

It was the russet season of autumn when leaves swirled over the gardens like flocks of birds. Wafting on the air came the tang of damp, bare earth, caught as the smell of a woman's naked flesh as her gown slips down to the floor after the ball.

On an evening during a reception held the previous spring, Madame d'Avancelles had replied to an imploring Monsieur de Croissard with the words: 'If I am to fall at all, my friend, it will certainly not be before the leaves do likewise. I've far too many things to do this summer to give it a thought.' He had remembered those daring words of hers spoken so provocatively and was now pressing his advantage. Each day he crept closer, gaining more and more of the bold beauty's heart until by this point her resistance seemed hardly more than symbolic.

Soon there was to be a great hunting party. The night before, Madame Berthe had said laughingly to the Baron: 'Tomorrow, Baron, if you manage to kill the beast I shall have something to give you.'

He was up at dawn reconnoitring where the wild boar

was wallowing. He accompanied his whips, setting out the order of the hunt in such a way that he should return from the field in triumph. When the horns sounded for the meet, he appeared in a well-cut hunting costume of scarlet and gold. With his upright, broad-chested figure and flashing eyes he glowed with good health and manly vigour.

The hunt moved off. The boar was raised and ran, followed by the baying hounds rushing through the undergrowth. The horses broke into a gallop, hurtling with their riders along the narrow forest paths while far behind the following carriages drove noiselessly over the softer verges.

Teasingly, Madame d'Avancelles kept the Baron at her side, slowing down to walking pace in an interminably long, straight avenue along which four rows of oaks arched vaultlike towards each other. Trembling with both desire and frustration he listened with one ear to the young woman's light badinage, the other pricked for the hunting horns and the sound of the hounds growing fainter by the minute.

'So you love me no longer,' she was saying.

'How can you say such a thing?' he replied.

'You do seem to be more interested in the hunt than in me,' she went on. He groaned. 'You do remember your own orders don't you? To kill the beast myself.'

'Indeed I do,' she added with great seriousness. 'Before my very eyes.' At this he quivered impatiently in the saddle, spurred on his eager horse and finally lost his patience.

'For God's sake, Madame, not if we stay here a minute longer.'

'That is how it has to be nevertheless,' she cried laughingly. 'Otherwise, you're out of luck.'

Then she spoke to him gently, leaning her hand on his arm and, as if absentmindedly, stroking his horse's mane. They had turned right on to a narrow path overhung with trees when, suddenly swerving to avoid one of their low branches, she leaned against him so closely that he felt her hair tickling his neck. He threw his arms around her and pressing his thick moustache to her forehead planted upon it a passionate kiss.

At first she was motionless, stunned by his ardour, then with a start she turned her head and, either by chance or design, her own delicate lips met his beneath their blond cascade. Then, out of either embarrassment or regret for the incident she spurred her horse on the flank and galloped swiftly away. For a long while they rode straight on together, without so much as exchanging a glance.

The hunt in full cry was close and the thickets seemed to shake, when suddenly, covered in blood and shaking off the hounds that clung to him, the boar went rushing past through the bushes. The Baron gave a triumphant laugh, cried 'Let him who loves me follow me!' and disappeared, swallowed up by the forest. When Madame d'Avancelles reached an open glade a few minutes later he was just getting up, covered with mud, his jacket torn and his hands bloody, while the animal lay full length on the ground with the Baron's knife plunged up to the hilt in its shoulder.

The quarry was cut by torchlight on that mild and melancholy night. The moon gilded the red flames of the torches which filled the air with pine smoke. The dogs, yelping and snapping, devoured the stinking innards of the boar while the beaters and the gentlemen, standing in a circle around the spoil, blew their horns with all their might. The flourish of the hunting horns rose into the night air above the woods. Its echoes fell and were lost in the distant valleys beyond, alarming nervous stags, a barking fox and small grey rabbits at play on the edge of the glades. Terrified night birds fluttered above the crazed pack while the women, excited a little by the violence and vulnerability surrounding these events, leaned a little heavily on the men's arms and, without waiting for the hounds to finish, drifted off with their partners down the many forest paths. Feeling languid after all the exhausting emotion of the day Madame d'Avancelles said to the Baron: 'Would you care for a turn in the park, my friend?'

He gave no answer, but trembling and unsteady with desire pulled her to him. Instantly they kissed and as they walked very slowly under the almost leafless trees through which moonlight filtered, their love, their desire and their need for each other was so intense that they almost sank down at the foot of a tree.

The horns had fallen silent and the exhausted hounds were sleeping by now in their kennels.

'Let us go back,' the young woman said. They returned.

Just as they reached the château and were about to enter, she murmured in a faint voice: 'I'm so tired, my friend, I'm going straight to bed.' As he opened his arms for one last kiss she fled, with the parting words: 'No . . . to sleep . . . but . . . let him who loves me follow me!'

An hour later when the whole sleeping château seemed dead to the world the Baron crept on tiptoe out of his room and scratched at the door of his friend. Receiving no reply he made to open it and found it unbolted.

She was leaning dreamily with her elbows on the window ledge. He threw himself at her knees which he showered with mad kisses through her nightdress. She said nothing, but ran her dainty fingers caressingly through the Baron's hair. Suddenly, as if coming to a momentous decision, she disengaged herself and whispered provocatively: 'Wait for me. I shall be back.' Her finger raised in shadow pointed to the far end of the room where loomed the vague white shape of her bed.

With wildly trembling hands he undressed quickly by feel and slipped between the cool sheets. He stretched out in bliss and almost forgot his friend as his weary body yielded to the linen's caress. Doubtless enjoying the strain on his patience, still she did not return. He closed his eyes in exquisitely pleasurable anticipation. His most cherished dream was about to come true. Little by little his limbs relaxed, as did his mind, where thoughts drifted, vague and indistinct. He succumbed at last to the power of great fatigue and finally fell asleep.

He slept the heavy, impenetrable sleep of the exhausted huntsman. He slept indeed till dawn. Then from a nearby tree through the still half-open window came the ringing cry of a cock. Startled awake, the Baron's eyes flew open. Finding himself, to his great surprise, in a strange bed and with a woman's body lying against his he remembered nothing and stammered as he struggled into consciousness: 'What? Where am I? What is it?'

At this, she, who had not slept a wink, looked at the puffy, red-eyed and dishevelled man at her side. She answered in the same dismissive tone she took with her husband. 'Nothing,' she said, 'it's a cock. Go back to sleep, Monsieur. It's nothing to do with you.'

Happiness

Dusk was falling at the time before the lamps were brought in at the villa which looked out on to the sea. Above it the sun, now out of sight, had left in its wake a sky of pink with a dusting of gold. The Mediterranean, without a ripple on its surface and gleaming still in the light of the dying day, lay ahead like a boundless sheet of polished metal.

To the right in the distance the black lace-edged silhouette of the mountains stood out against the pale mauve of the sunset. The talk was on the age-old subject of love and the same was being said as had been said countless times before. In the gentle, melancholy twilight the conversation was leisurely and wistful. The word 'love', constantly repeated now by a strong, masculine voice, now in the lighter tones of a woman, seemed to fill the little drawing room, its spirit floating and hovering birdlike over the scene.

Was it possible to stay in love over a long period of years? Some people said yes, others no. Examples were given, definitions attempted, cases cited. Everyone, men and women alike, seemed moved by the memories, some disturbing, some long since buried, which came flooding back. Each spoke with great feeling and conviction about the most commonplace yet the most important aspect of life: the mysterious bond of affection between two human beings.

Suddenly one of the group who had been looking out into the distance, shouted: 'Oh look! Over there! What on earth is that?'

Rising from the ocean on the far horizon a huge grey mass could be seen. The women left their chairs and gazed uncomprehendingly at this amazing phenomenon which none of them had ever seen before.

Someone said: 'It's Corsica! Just once or twice a year you can see it. The atmospheric conditions have to be absolutely right, and that doesn't often happen. The air has to be completely transparent. Otherwise mists form and normally at that distance they obscure it.'

Mountain crests could just about be distinguished and some people thought they could see snowy summits. Everyone was amazed and a little disturbed, even frightened by the sudden appearance of this land, rising like a phantom from the deep. It was the sort of strange sight explorers such as Columbus must have seen in days of old.

Just then an elderly gentleman, who had not spoken before, said: 'As a matter of fact that island appearing suddenly like that before us as if to take part in our discussion has reminded me of something quite extraordinary.

It was there that I once came across a wonderful example of constant and unbelievably happy love.'

'Five years ago I was travelling in Corsica. That wild island is more distant and unknown to us than America, even though she can sometimes be seen as she is today from our very own French shores. Imagine a world still in primeval chaos. Imagine a great eruption of mountains separated by narrow ravines full of raging torrents. Not a single plain, just huge waves of granite, great reefs of land covered with bush and tall forests of chestnut and pine.

It is virgin soil, uncultivated and deserted apart from the occasional village which looks like a pile of rocks perched on top of a hill. No culture, no industry, no art. You never come across so much as a carved piece of wood or stone; no trace, however sketchy, of any desire on the part of early man here to create style or beauty. This is the most striking aspect of the place. It's a magnificent, rough land, utterly indifferent to the attraction of form which we call art.

You've got, on the one hand, Italy where every palazzo is full of masterpieces and which is itself a masterpiece. There, marble, wood, bronze, iron and every other kind of metal and stone are transformed to reflect the genius of man. Even the most insignificant of objects discovered in the ruins demonstrates a spiritual yearning. We all love Italy, we cherish the place precisely because it attests to, is visible living proof of, the effort, the greatness, the power and the triumph of creativity in man.

And directly opposite you have Corsica, which has remained as it was from the very beginning. Its inhabitants live in their crude habitations, oblivious of everything but the very basic necessities of life and family vendettas. It has retained both the qualities and the defects of primitive man: violence, hatred and mindless savagery. Yet the people there are hospitable, generous, loyal and innocent. They will open their doors to passing strangers and offer unconditional friendship at the first sign of camaraderie.

For a month I had been wandering about this splendid country, feeling myself at the ends of the earth. Not a single inn, no cafés, no roads. It is only by mule track that you can reach the hamlets clinging to the sides of the mountains which look down into tortuous gulleys. From these in the evening a constant clamour rises which is the deep, distant roar of rapids. You knock on someone's door. You ask for a night's lodging and food till the next day. You sit down at a modest board and sleep under a humble roof. The following day you shake the hand offered to you by your host who will have accompanied you as far as the village boundary.

It happened that one night after ten hours' walking, I came across a lonely little dwelling at the bottom of a narrow valley two or three miles inland. The two steep sides of the mountain, covered as they were with bush,

fallen rocks and tall trees, enclosed this sombre, lugubri-
ous ravine like two dark walls. Around the cottage were
a few vines, a little garden and, further off, a few chestnut
trees – more than enough to live on in this impoverished
land. The elderly woman who received me looked somewhat severe, but unusually clean. The man who had been
sitting in a rush-bottomed chair got up to greet me, then
sat down again in silence. His companion said to me: 'Do
excuse him. He's deaf now, I'm afraid. He's eighty-two.'
She spoke proper French, which surprised me.

"You're not from Corsica, then, I gather?"

"No, we're from the Continent originally. But we've
lived here for fifty years."

A feeling of fear and anguish gripped me at the
thought of fifty years spent in this dark hole so far from
towns and people. An old shepherd came to join us and
we sat down to a single course – a thick soup of cabbage,
potato and bacon.

When this brief meal was over I went to sit outside the
front door. I was in low spirits as I contemplated the bleak
landscape and was saddened as travellers sometimes are
on certain evenings in a desolate place. You get the feeling
that everything – human existence and the universe
itself – is about to come to an end. You're suddenly struck
by the misery of life, the isolation in which we all live, the
nothingness of it all and the desperate loneliness in hearts
deluded by dreams until death.

The old woman joined me. Even in the pessimistic

mood I was in I could feel keen curiosity stirring within me.

"So you're from France, are you?" she said.

"Yes, I'm here for pleasure."

"Are you from Paris, by any chance?"

"No, from Nancy."

This news seemed to have an extraordinary effect on her. It wasn't anything you could put your finger on, just an impression I got.

She continued, speaking very slowly: "From Nancy, did you say?"

The man appeared at the door, impassive as the deaf inevitably are.

She went on: 'Never mind. He can't hear.' Then, after a few moments: "So, do you know many people in Nancy?"

"Oh yes. Practically everybody."

"The Saint-Allaizes?"

"Very well. They were friends of my father."

"What's your name, did you say?"

I gave it. She stared at me, then, in the low voice with which we speak our memories, she said: "I know that name very well. Very well indeed. What about the Brise-mares, what's become of them, then?"

"All dead now, I'm afraid."

"Ah! And the Sirmonts, do you know them?"

"Yes. The latest Sirmont's now a general."

This time she spoke in a voice trembling with emotion, anguish and some other indescribable but powerful feeling. It seemed like an almost religious desire to confess, to say everything, to talk about things which she had been bottling up for years and about people the mere mention of whose name had such an overwhelming effect upon her.

"Yes, Henri de Sirmont. We're talking about my brother."

I raised my eyes and looked at her in astonishment. Then all of a sudden it hit me.

The whole affair had in its day scandalized the entire aristocracy of Lorraine. A beautiful, rich young girl had eloped with a non-commissioned officer from her father's regiment. He was a handsome fellow of peasant stock who looked well in the blue uniform of the Hussars. She had no doubt noticed him on parade, picked him out from all the others and fallen in love with him. But how she had managed to speak to him, how they had been able to see and get to know each other, how she had dared let him know that she loved him no one was ever to know.

No one suspected a thing and it happened quite without warning. One night when the soldier's tour of duty had come to an end he disappeared with her. They were hunted but never found. No news was ever received from them and eventually it was as if they were dead.

And here she was living in this sinister valley.

Now it was my turn to speak: "I remember very well. You must be Mademoiselle Suzanne."

She nodded. Tears had welled up in her eyes and were

now coursing down her cheeks. Then, indicating the old man standing motionless on the threshold she said: "That's him."

I realized that she was still in love with him. She still saw him with the same eyes as always.

"Well at least you've been happy?" I asked.

"Oh yes! Very happy! He has made me very happy! I've never had a single regret."

I gazed at her, feeling moved, astonished and marvelling at the power of love. This wealthy girl had followed a peasant and become a peasant herself. She had adapted herself to this basic, charmless existence with no luxuries and no comfort of any sort. She had conformed to his simple ways. And still she loved him. In her bonnet and her thick cotton skirt she had become a country wife. She ate a broth of cabbage, bacon and potato from an earthenware bowl off a scrubbed wooden table, sitting on a simple rush-bottomed chair. At night she slept beside him on a straw mattress.

Nothing else mattered except him. She had missed none of the finery, the costly materials, the elegance, the comfortable chairs, the fragrant warmth of the tapestry-hung bedrooms, the restful, welcoming softness of the bedding. She had never needed anything apart from him. He was all she wanted. As long as he was there she was happy. Early on she had given up the life she was used to and the people who had brought her up and loved her. She had come on her own with him to this wild ravine.

He had been everything to her; all that she desired, all she dreamed of, all she always wished and ever hoped for. He had filled her life to the brim with happiness. She could not have been more content.

All night long I heard the harsh breathing of the old soldier on his pallet with, beside him, the woman who had followed him so far. I thought what a strange yet simple adventure it must have been to create such complete happiness with so little.

I left at dawn having shaken hands with the old married couple.'

The man telling the story had come to the end of his tale. One woman said, 'It's quite obvious she had no standards, this woman. She had very simple, basic needs, easily met. She must have been an idiot.'

Another said slowly, 'What does it matter? She was happy, that's what counts!'

And now on the far distant horizon the vast shadow faded into the night, sliding gently into the sea, and with it Corsica, which had appeared as if to tell in person the story of the two simple lovers welcomed to her shores.

Madame Husson's Rose King

We had just come through Gisors where I had woken at the sound of porters' voices shouting out the name of the station. I was just about to slide gently back to sleep again when a violent jerk of the train sent me flying into the lap of a stout lady sitting opposite. One of the engine wheels had broken and the engine itself was now lying across the track. The tender and the luggage van, also derailed, lay next to the dying creature as it expired, wheezing and croaking, whistling and spitting the while. Like a horse collapsed in the street with its chest and flanks heaving and nostrils steaming, the whole shuddering body was totally incapable of struggling upright again.

The train had barely got up steam when the accident happened and there were neither fatalities nor casualties apart from a few cases of concussion. We all looked sadly at the poor crippled iron beast incapable now of carrying us an inch further. It was going to obstruct the rail for some considerable time since more than likely an emergency locomotive from Paris would have to be sent for.

It was ten o'clock in the morning and I decided immediately to walk back in the direction of Gisors where I might possibly find some lunch. As I walked along the track I thought to myself, 'Gisors . . . Gisors . . . don't I know somebody in . . . haven't I got a friend living in Gisors?' Suddenly the name Albert Marambot flashed into my mind. He was an old schoolfriend of mine whom I had not seen for at least twelve years and who was now practising medicine at Gisors. He had often written asking me to stay. I had always said I would one day, but never had. Now was the time to take him up on it.

I asked the first person I met where Dr Marambot lived and got an immediate response in a Normandy drawl. He lived on the rue Dauphine. And there indeed, on the door pointed out to me, I could see a brass plate engraved with the name of my old chum. I rang. The young, blonde servant girl who answered looked a little dim and kept repeating, ' 'E's not in.' However, in the background I could hear the clink of glasses and cutlery. 'Hey Marambot!' I shouted. A door opened and a fat man with whiskers appeared, holding a table napkin in his hand and looking not best pleased.

I would never have recognized him. He looked at least forty-five, and in one second I could see reflected in his face all the dullness and tedium of provincial life. In a single flash as instantaneous as my own handshake I knew everything about his way of life, his approach to existence, the sort of mentality he would have developed and his views on the state of the world. I could visualize the lengthy meals contributing to his paunch, the after-dinner snoozes in a cognac-induced haze, the cursory examinations he would give patients while his thoughts strayed to the chicken roasting on the spit at home. I could hear all the conversations about food, about cider, about brandy and about wine; about the best way to cook a certain dish, to blend a certain sauce. All was revealed to me as I took in his florid complexion, his thick lips and his dull, lacklustre eyes.

'You don't recognize me, do you?' I said. 'I'm Raoul Aubertin.'

He opened his arms wide and nearly crushed me to death. His first words were: 'You haven't had lunch yet, I hope?'

'No.'

'Wonderful! I'm just sitting down to an excellent trout. Come and join me.'

Five minutes later I was seated opposite him and tucking in to lunch.

'So you never married?' I asked.

'Good heavens no!'

'And you like it here?'

'Oh yes! Always busy, always something to do. Patients, friends. I eat well. I'm in good health. Lots of good laughs. Good hunting. What more could a man desire? Not much, in my view!'

'And you don't get bored living in such a small place?'

'Not for a minute. Plenty going on always. Small town's just like a large one, I'd say. There's less variety in the way of entertainments but then each one becomes more exciting as a result. You know fewer people but you see them oftener. When you know every window in a small place, each individual one is more interesting than a whole streetful in Paris. You can have a very nice time, a very, very nice time indeed in a small town, you know. I mean, take this one for example, Gisors, I know its history backwards, from the earliest times to the present day. And I tell you it's absolutely fascinating.'

'Are you from Gisors yourself?'

'Not Gisors, no. I'm from Gournay. That's its sister town, and its rival. Gournay is to Gisors what Lucullus was to Cicero. In Gournay, the big thing is food. People refer to the inhabitants as the "Gournay Guzzlers". Gisors looks down its nose at Gournay. But of course the people of Gournay laugh at Gisors. It's absolutely hilarious!'

I realized that what I was eating was truly exquisite: soft-boiled eggs enveloped in a slightly chilled, herb-flavoured meat jelly. Smacking my lips appreciatively I said, 'This really is very good indeed.'

My host smiled.

'Two things you've got to have: proper meat jelly – not so easy to find as you might think – and decent eggs. Decent eggs are few and far between, you know. You want one with a slightly reddish yolk, nice and tasty. I've got two separate hen houses as a matter of fact. One for laying hens. One for chickens for the table. I give my layers a special feed. I'm very particular. With eggs, just as with chicken meat and of course with beef and lamb, with milk, with everything in fact, you've got to be able to taste the sap, the quintessence of what the animal itself has been feeding on. We'd have much better food if we just bore that in mind a bit more.'

I laughed. 'Keen on food then, are you?'

'Good God, only idiots aren't keen on food! Being keen on food is like being keen on the arts, keen on education, keen on poetry, what have you! The sense of taste, my dear chap, is as delicate a sense, as sensitive and as reliable a sense as sight and hearing. To be deprived of taste is to lose an exquisite faculty, the capacity to discern quality in food just as in literature or in works of art. If you don't have that, you're deprived of an essential sense, one of the ones that constitute human superiority over animals. Without it, you'd be one of the many insensitive, lumpen, brutish kinds of creatures our race is generally made up of. To have an insensitive palate is like having a dull mind. A man who can't tell the difference between a crayfish and a lobster, say, or a herring – that wonderful multi-flavoured fish which contains every known taste of sea-life – a man who can't tell a herring from a mackerel, a Crassane pear from a Duchesse, is like a man who can't distinguish between Balzac and Eugène Sue, between a Beethoven symphony and a military march, or who can't make a distinction between the Apollo of Belvedere and the statue of General Blanmont.'

'Who's General Blanmont?'

'Oh, of course you wouldn't know. You're not from

Gisors, obviously. Did I tell you the inhabitants of Gisors are known as the "Glorious of Gisors"? Never was the term more appropriate. But let's finish lunch first. Then I'll tell you all about the town as we go round it. From time to time he stopped talking to take a long slow sip of his half-glass of wine which he looked at with tenderness as he replaced it on the table.

He was quite a comical sight with his napkin knotted around his neck, his red cheeks, his gleaming eyes and his whiskers now framing beautifully his ever-busy mouth. He made me eat till I was fit to burst. Then, since I needed to get back to the station, he grabbed my arm and guided me through the streets of the town. A fine example of the provincial style, it was dominated by a fortress, one of the most curious military structures in the whole of France. It overlooked a long, green valley on whose pastureland lumbering Norman cattle grazed and chewed the cud.

'Gisors,' said the doctor 'population approximately 4,000, situated on the borders of the Eure, is mentioned as early as in Caesar's *Commentaries*: Caesaris ostium, then Caesartium, Caesortium, Gisortium, Gisors. I shan't take you up to the Roman camp, the ruins of which are visible to this day.'

Laughing, I replied: 'My dear fellow, it looks to me as though you're suffering from a disease which as a medical man you might be interested in. It's called parochialism.'

He stopped in his tracks.

'Parochialism, my friend, is nothing other than natural patriotism. I love my house, my town, and by extension my province because it still upholds the traditions of my village. In the same way I love the frontier and am happy to defend it should a neighbour encroach upon it, because my own house is threatened and because the frontier, though it may be unfamiliar ground to me, represents the path to my province. In other words I'm a Norman through and through. I might happen to have a grudge now against the Germans. I might want to get revenge on them. But I don't actually hate them. I don't loathe them as instinctively as I do the English, who are my real, my traditional enemy. It's the English who set foot on the soil of my ancestors and raped and pillaged here from time immemorial. The aversion I have for those deceitful people is something given to me at birth by my father . . . Oh, by the way, here's the statue of the general.'

'Which general was that?'

'General Blanmont, of course! We had to have a statue. We're not called the Glorious of Gisors for nothing! So we found General Blanmont. Look over here.'

He dragged me towards the window of a bookshop in which fifteen or so volumes bound in yellow, black and red immediately drew the eye. The titles made me giggle. They read:

Gisors, its Past and its Future, by Monsieur X, member of several learned societies

Guy de Maupassant

The History of Gisors, by the Abbé A.
Gisors from Caesar's Day to Our Own, by Monsieur B,
     proprietor
Gisors and District, by Dr C.D.
The Glories of Gisors, by some researcher or other.

'My dear fellow,' Marambot went on, 'do you know not a year goes by, not one year without the publication of some new history of Gisors. We have some twenty-three altogether.'

'And what exactly are these glories of Gisors?' I asked.

'Oh, there are so many! I couldn't list them all. I'll just tell you the main ones. First of all, we have General Blanmont, then the Baron Davillier, the famous ceramicist who went on expeditions to Spain and the Balearic Islands and brought back wonderful examples, collectors' pieces of Hispano-Arabic pottery. In literature, we've got the late, great journalist Charles Brainne, and among those very much alive and kicking we have the eminent editor-in-chief of the *Nouvelliste de Rouen*, Charles Lapierre . . . and many, many more . . .'

We were going up a long, slightly sloping street, the entire length of which was now being warmed by the June sun from which most of the inhabitants had escaped indoors. All of a sudden, at the other end of this street a man appeared, staggering and obviously drunk. His head was stuck forward as he lurched, with unsteady legs and his arms dangling on either side of his body, in a series of three, six or ten little steps at a time, followed by a rest. When his brief burst of energy took him into the middle of the road he stopped dead and teetered, hesitating between collapse and a fresh surge. Then off he went at a tangent again. He ran straight into the wall of a house and seemed for a moment glued there as if he expected to be drawn in by suction. Then, with a shake he turned round and stared fixedly ahead, slack-jawed, his eyes blinking against the glare of the sun. Jerking his back off the wall he set off once more. A scrawny little yellow mongrel followed him, barking, stopping and starting in accompaniment.

'Well, well,' said Marambot, 'there's Madame Husson's Rose King.'

I was extremely surprised and asked: 'Madame Husson's Rose King? What do you mean by that?'

The doctor began to laugh.

'Oh, it's what we call drunkards round here. It's an old story that's become a bit of a legend locally. Even though every word of it is true.'

'Good story?'

'Very funny indeed.'

'Tell me then.'

'With pleasure.'

'In this town, there used to live a very proper, correct old lady who was a great believer in virtue. Her name was Madame Husson. These are real names that I'm telling you – I'm not making them up. Madame Husson was particularly involved with good works, helping the poor, encouraging the worthy, that sort of thing. She was small and took tiny little steps. She wore a black silk wig and was on very good terms with the Almighty in the person of the abbé Malou. She abhorred vice of any kind but particularly the one the Church refers to as lust. The idea of any kind of intimacy before marriage incensed her. She used to be beside herself at the thought of it.

Just about this time there were a lot of Rose Queens being crowned on the outskirts of Paris, and it occurred to Madame Husson that it might be a good idea for Gisors to have one of its own. She told the abbé Malou about her idea and he immediately drew up a list of candidates. Now Madame Husson had in service with her an elderly maid called Françoise, who was equally strict in her views. As soon as the priest had gone, her mistress called her and said: "Now look, Françoise, here's a list of the girls Monsieur le curé recommends for their virtue. Try and find out what other people think of them, will you?"

Françoise applied herself to the task with vigour. She gathered together every scrap of gossip and tittle-tattle she could find and every hint of suspicion, however small. In case she should forget any details, she wrote them all down in her household expense book where, having adjusted her spectacles on her thin nose, Madame Husson would read:

Bread	four sous
Milk	two sous
Butter	eight sous

Malvina Lavesque seen out last ear with Mathurin Poilu.

Leg of lamb	twenty five sous
Salt	one sou

Rosalie Vatinel seen with Césaire Piénoir in Riboulet wood by Madame Onésine, laundress and presser on twentieth july at dusc.

Radish	one sou
Vinegar	two sous
Sorrel salt	two sous

Joséphine Durdent tho not believed to have fallen non-obstant in corraspondance with the Oportun boy now in servise in Rouen and he send her by diligence a present of a bonnet.

No girl emerged from this rigorous inquiry intact. Françoise asked everybody – neighbours, tradesmen, the infant-school teacher and the sisters at the convent school. She sniffed out the smallest scrap of information. And since there isn't a girl in the world totally untouched by gossip, not a single young girl could be found in the entire district with no hint of scandal attached to her name.

Madame Husson, however, was determined that the Rose Queen of Gisors, like Caesar's wife, should be entirely above suspicion. She was staggered and appalled by what she read in her maid's expense book and began to despair of ever finding a suitable girl. The catchment area was enlarged to include a greater number of neighbouring villages. Still no one could be found. The Mayor was consulted. His own protégées also failed the test as did those of Dr Barbesol, despite the rigorously scientific nature of his assurances.

Then one day on her return from the shops Françoise said to her mistress: "You know, Madame, if you want to crown somebody local, it's going to have to be Isidore."

This set Madame Husson thinking.

She knew Isidore very well. He was the son of Virginie who kept the greengrocer's shop. His amazing celibacy was now Gisors' pride and joy. It was also an interesting topic of conversation throughout the town and a source of great amusement to the girls, who teased him mercilessly about it. He was past twenty now, tall and gangling, shy and a bit slow in his manner. He helped his mother in the business and spent most of his time sitting on a chair near the shop door preparing the fruit and vegetables for display.

He was scared witless by girls and immediately lowered his gaze if one of them gave him a smile when she came into the shop. This well-known timidity of his made him the easy butt of every joke in town. Anything vaguely rude or risqué made him blush so quickly that Dr Barbesol called him his modesty thermometer. His neighbours took malicious delight in speculating whether he knew anything or not. What was it exactly which affected the greengrocer's son so deeply? Was it plain indignation at the necessarily messy contact required by love for its full flowering? Or was it shame for his ignorance about something mysterious and unknown?

Little urchins would run up and down in front of the shop yelling obscenities, simply to see him lower his gaze. Girls passed back and forth, whispering wicked things which would force him to retreat indoors. The bolder ones teased him openly for the hell of it, asking him for dates and making terrible suggestions.

Anyway, as I say, Madame Husson was giving it much thought. It was certainly true that Isidore was a remarkable, not to say a famous, example of virtue. Totally unimpeachable. No one, not even the most sceptical, even the most suspicious mind could cast any doubt whatsoever on Isidore's complete moral integrity. He had never once been seen in a café and never out in the street at night. He went to bed at eight and got up at four. He was a pearl among men. Perfection itself.

Still Madame Husson hesitated. The idea of substituting a Rose King for a Rose Queen still worried and dismayed her a little. She decided to consult the abbé Malou.

The abbé replied: "What is it you wish to reward, Madame? Virtue, is it not? Virtue pure and simple. In which case, what does it matter if it be male or female? Virtue is eternal. It transcends birth and gender. It is *Virtue*."

Thus encouraged, Madame Husson went to see the mayor. He was in total agreement.

"We shall have a beautiful ceremony," he said. "Then another year if we find a woman as worthy as Isidore we shall crown a woman. I would go so far as to say that this could act as a lesson to Nanterre. *We* do not exclude. Let *us* be the ones who welcome merit of every kind."

Isidore when he was told blushed deeply and appeared very happy. The coronation date was fixed for 15 August, the Feast of the Virgin Mary, dedicated also to the Emperor Napoleon. The municipality decided to make a big splash on this occasion and accordingly a platform was built on what became known as the Coronation Gardens, a lovely extension of the old fortress's ramparts which I'll show you in a minute.

In a natural reversal of public opinion Isidore's virtue, hitherto ridiculed and mocked in some circles, became overnight universally acknowledged as enviable and respectable, especially now that it was carrying off a prize of 500 francs as well as a savings book. Not to mention all the honour and glory. The girls were sorry they had been so coarse and vulgar. A little smile of satisfaction now played on Isidore's lips, reflecting his inner happiness.

On the eve of 15 August the entire rue Dauphine was decked with flags and bunting . . . Oh! I forgot to tell you why this street is called the rue Dauphine. Apparently the Dauphine, I'm not sure which one, was visiting Gisors one day. She had been kept in the public eye for so long accepting all the formal presentations and formalities that suddenly, in the middle of the procession through the town, she stopped in front of one of the houses on this street and cried: "Oh what a lovely house! How I should love to visit it! Pray who is the owner?" The owner was named and found and, covered in glory and confusion, brought before the princess. She got out of her carriage, entered the house, declared her intention to inspect its every nook and cranny and even asked to be left closeted in one of the upstairs rooms by herself for a few minutes. When she re-emerged, the people, flattered by the honour shown to a citizen of Gisors, yelled, 'Vive la Dauphine!' However, a local wag composed a little ditty and the street was renamed after her royal highness's title. It went:

> With no holy water
> The king's lovely daughter
> Baptized it alone
> With some of her own.

But I digress. To get back to Isidore. Flowers were strewn all along the route of the procession, just as on the day of the Fête Dieu. The National Guard was in attendance under its commander-in-chief, Major Desbarres, a stalwart old veteran of the *grande armée*. Next to the framed Cross of Honour given to him by the emperor himself, he used to proudly display the beard of a cossack sliced from its owner's chin in one fell swoop of Desbarres' sword during the retreat from Russia. The corps under his command were some of the crack troops of the entire province. The famous Gisors Grenadiers were called in on every important occasion within a radius of at least fifteen to twenty miles. It's said that King Louis-Philippe, as he was reviewing the troops of the Eure, stopped in amazement when he came to the Gisors company and cried, "Oh, who are these fine grenadiers?" "They are from Gisors", the general replied, at which the king is alleged to have commented, "I might have known it!"

So there was Desbarres leading his men behind a military band to escort Isidore from his mother's shop. After a little fanfare had been played under his windows, the Rose King himself appeared on the threshold. He was dressed from head to toe in white drill and wore a straw hat, on the brim of which lay a little circlet of orange-blossom. The question of costume had been a source of great worry to Madame Husson. She was torn between the sober black jacket of First Communion and a whole suit of pure white. It was Françoise, her adviser, who made her plump for the white suit, saying it would make the Rose King look as graceful as a swan.

From behind him his guardian angel and godmother, Madame Husson, appeared in triumph. She took his arm to proceed forward and the Mayor positioned himself on the Rose King's other side. The band played a drum-roll, Major Desbarres shouted, "Present arms!" and the procession moved off towards the church amidst a vast crowd of people who had come from outlying communes for miles around. After a brief Mass was said and a touching address given by the abbé Malou, they proceeded again, this time towards the Coronation Gardens where a banquet was to be served in a marquee. Before taking his seat the Mayor made a speech. I have learned it by heart, it's so beautiful.

> Young man [he said], a worthy lady of charity, beloved of the poor and respected by the rich, Madame Husson, to whom I offer thanks on behalf of the entire community, has conceived the idea – the happy and munificent idea – of founding in this town a prize for virtue intended to act as a precious encouragement to the inhabitants of our beautiful region.
>
> You, young man, are the first to be elected, the first to be crowned in this dynasty of wisdom and charity. Your name will head the list of the most meritorious. Your life, mark this well, your entire life must follow in the spirit of this most auspicious of beginnings. Today, in the presence of this noble woman who rewards your conduct; in the presence of our soldier-citizens who took up arms to defend the honour of those such as you; in the presence of this congregation gathered here in love to acclaim you, or rather, virtue made manifest in you, you make a solemn pledge with this town and with all of us here to follow unto death the excellent example you have hitherto shown in youth. Never forget, young man, you are the first seed to be sown in the soil of hope. Bring to us the harvest we have come to expect of you.

The Mayor took three steps forward towards Isidore who was now sobbing, opened his arms wide and embraced him warmly. The Rose King wept, he knew not why, with mixed emotions of pride and a sort of simple joy. The Mayor placed in one of his hands a silken purse in which solid gold clinked – 500 francs in gold! Having placed in Isidore's other hand a savings book, he declared in a solemn voice: "All honour, glory and wealth to virtue!"

Major Desbarres cried "Bravo!", the grenadiers echoed him in chorus and the people burst into applause. It was now Madame Husson's turn to wipe tears from her eyes. They then took their places at the table where the banquet was being served. It was both magnificent and interminable. Course after course was brought. Yellow cider and red wine flowed in and out of convivial glasses and reached appreciative throats. The clatter of crockery, the sound of voices and that of music in the background provided a constant, resonant buzz which faded as it rose into the sky where swallows now flew.

From time to time Madame Husson adjusted her black silk wig, which had a tendency to keel over and remain beached on her ear. She chatted amicably with the abbé Malou while the Mayor in a state of high excitement talked politics with the major. Isidore ate and drank as he never had before! He took helpings and second helpings of everything on offer and realized for the first time how wonderful it is to feel one's stomach fill with things that have already tasted heavenly in the mouth. He had slyly undone the buckle of his trouser-belt which was straining under the pressure of his rapidly distending belly. Silent now, and a little worried about a wine stain on his white drill jacket, he stopped eating and brought to his lips a glass which stayed there for some time as he slowly savoured its contents.

It was time now for the toasts. There were many, each applauded with great enthusiasm. Night was beginning to fall and they had been at table since noon. Already, over the valley fine, milky mists were forming as the rivers and the meadows put on their gauzy nightgowns. The sun sank slowly towards the horizon, cattle were lowing in the distant hazy pastures and people were beginning to amble down home to Gisors. The procession broke into little groups for the return leg and Madame Husson, having taken Isidore's arm, was giving him much urgent and no doubt invaluable advice. Finally they arrived at the greengrocery door and the Rose King was deposited at his mother's house.

She, however, was not yet back. Having been invited by relatives to a family celebration of her son's triumph she had followed the procession as far as the banqueting marquee then gone on to lunch at her sister's. Isidore was therefore on his own in the shop as night fell. His head spinning with pride and the effects of the wine, he sat on a chair and looked about him. Carrots, cabbages and onions filled the enclosed space with their strong earthy, vegetable smell. Mingling with it was the sweet, pervasive fragrance of strawberries and the fleeting scent that wafted from a basket of peaches. The Rose King took one and bit into it eagerly even though his belly was as round as a barrel. Then in a sudden surge of joy he leapt to his feet and began to dance. As he did so, something clinked in his jacket. Surprised, he plunged his hands into the pockets and from one drew out the purse containing the 500 francs. He had completely forgotten them. Five hundred francs! A fortune! He poured the louis on to the counter and, with a loving gesture, spread them out so that he could see them in all their glory. There were twenty-five coins in all. Twenty-five solid gold coins! All gold! In the gathering darkness they gleamed on the wood as he counted and recounted them over and over again. He put a finger on each murmuring, "One, two, three, four, five, hundred; six, seven, eight, nine, ten, two hundred." Then, putting them back in the purse, he stowed it safely away in his pocket again.

We will never know and who could ever tell what a terrible struggle between good and evil then took place in the Rose King's soul. What violent attack did Satan make upon him? What wicked temptation did he plant in this timid, virgin soul? What ideas, what suggestions, what desires did the Devil invent for the chosen one? Who knows? But Madame Husson's golden boy grabbed his hat with the little coronet of orange-blossom still resting on its brim. Slipping out through the back door he disappeared into the night.

Having been informed that her son had returned, Virginie the greengrocer came back at once and found the house empty. Initially unconcerned, after an hour had passed she started making inquiries. Her neighbours in the rue Dauphine had seen Isidore come home and not seen him go out again. They began to look for him. In vain. Worried now, the greengrocer ran to the Mayor's house. All the Mayor knew was that the Rose King had been escorted safely home.

Madame Husson had just gone to bed when the news was brought to her that her protégé had disappeared. She immediately put on her black silk wig again, got up and went to Virginie's herself. Virginie, a simple and emotional soul, was crying her eyes out surrounded by her cabbages, carrots and onions.

It was feared he might have had an accident. What sort, they wondered? Major Desbarres alerted the police who made a search of the entire town. On the road to Pontoise they found the little coronet of orange-blossom. It was placed on the table around which the authorities were now deliberating. The Rose King must have been the victim of some practical joke or, worse, of someone acting out of jealousy. What means had been employed to kidnap the innocent boy and what was the motive behind the kidnapping? Exhausted by the search they all went to bed, leaving Virginie to wait in tears alone.

The following night when the diligence returned from Paris, Gisors learned to its horror that its Rose King had flagged the coach down not 200 metres outside the parish boundary. He had got in, paid for his seat with a golden louis for which he was given change, and had got down in the very centre of the big city.

Feelings ran high at home. Letters were exchanged between the Mayor and the Paris chief of police but no further news came. Day followed day until finally a week passed. Then, out early one morning Dr Barbesol noticed a man sitting on someone's doorstep. He was dressed in a grey suit and, with his head propped up against the wall of the house, was fast asleep. The doctor approached and recognized the man as Isidore. He tried to wake him but failed. The former Rose King was in a worryingly deep, impenetrable slumber. The doctor was puzzled and called for help to carry the young man to Boncheval, the pharmacist. As they lifted him up an empty bottle rolled out from underneath him. Sniffing it, the doctor declared that it had held brandy, which was useful to know as they tried to bring him round. Eventually they succeeded.

Isidore was drunk. Sodden with drink in fact. After a week-long binge he was a complete wreck. His beautiful white drill suit was now a greyish yellow, filthy, torn, and covered in grease and stains; his breath and his entire body stank to high heaven of all the squalor and mess he had wallowed in for all that time.

He was washed, lectured and locked indoors for four days. He seemed ashamed and contrite. His purse containing the 500 francs had disappeared as had the savings book and even his silver watch, a precious heirloom bequeathed to him by his father the fruiterer.

On the fifth day he ventured out into the rue Dauphine. Curious looks followed him as he walked past the houses, head down, glancing furtively about him. He disappeared as he left town, making for the valley beyond. Two hours later he reappeared, giggling and bouncing from one wall to the other.

He never went back on the straight and narrow.

His mother kicked him out and he became a carter, driving coal trucks for Poigrisel and Co. – still in business today, as a matter of fact. His notoriety spread far and wide. As far away as Évreux people talked about Madame Husson's Rose King and it's become the local term for a drunkard.

All of which just goes to show – no charitable act ever goes entirely to waste.'

Dr Marambot rubbed his hands together as he came to the end of his story. I asked him if he had ever known the Rose King personally.

'Indeed I did. I had the honour of closing his eyes for the last time.'

'What did he die of?'

'Delirium tremens, of course.'

We had reached the old fortress, a mass of ruins now dominated by two towers, one called Saint Thomas of Canterbury's Tower and the other Prisoner's Tower. Marambot told me how this prisoner had managed, using a nail and the position of the sun as it filtered through an arrow-slit, to cover the entire surface of the walls of his cell with carvings.

I then learned that Clotaire II had given the town of Gisors to his cousin, the holy Bishop Romain of Rouen; that Gisors had ceased to be the capital of the Vexin region after the treaty of Saint-Clair-sur-Epte; that the town occupies the most strategically important position for this particular part of France and that accordingly it had been taken and re-taken times without number. Under orders from Guillaume the Red, the famous military engineer Robert de Bellesme had built a strong fortress there which was later attacked by Louis the Fat, then by various Norman barons; it had been defended by Robert de Candos and finally ceded to Louis the Fat by Geoffroy Plantagenet; then it was taken by the English as a result of a Templar betrayal; it was disputed by Philippe-Auguste and Richard Coeur de Lion, burned by Edward III of England who failed to take the castle; it was taken again by the English in 1419 and later bequeathed to Charles VII by Richard Marbury; taken once more by the Duke of Cabria, occupied by the Ligue, lived in by Henri IV, etc., etc., etc.

Marambot was now well into his stride.

'The bloody English, I tell you! What a bunch of drunks they are, my friend. They're all Rose Kings over there, the hypocrites!'

Then after a moment's silence he stretched out an arm in the direction of the narrow river gleaming in the pastureland below.

'Did you know, by the way, that Henry Monnier was one of the keenest anglers ever to fish from the banks of the Epte?'

'I didn't, actually.'

'And Bouffé, my dear chap, Bouffé, the stained-glass artist. He did some work here, too.'

'You don't say!'

'He certainly did. I'm really amazed at how little you know about the world!'

Who Knows?

I

My God! I can't believe it! At last, at long last, I am actually going to put down in black and white what happened to me! That's if I am able! If I dare! The whole story is so weird, so impossible to explain, so . . . crazy!

If I were not absolutely certain of what I saw and sure that there is no gap in the chain of events I am about to relate, if I were not totally convinced that there is no possibility of a mistake about what happened, I would simply think it was a hallucination or that I had been fooled by some sort of strange illusion. And when all is said and done, who knows anyway?

I am at present in a psychiatric clinic but I came here voluntarily as a precautionary measure because I was afraid. Only one other human being knows my history and that is the doctor here. I am going to write it down, though quite why, I am not sure. Perhaps to get it off my chest. The weight of it on my mind all the time is practically unbearable. It's a waking nightmare. These are the facts.

*

I have always been something of a loner, a bit dreamy, you might say, but well-meaning, unambitious, with no particular animosity towards my fellow human beings and fairly content with my lot. I have always lived alone because of a certain creeping unease I feel in the presence of other people. I don't know how to explain it. I am not averse to seeing people – I mean, I go out and eat with friends and so forth but if I feel they have been near me for any prolonged period of time, even the closest begin to get so much on my nerves that I have this overwhelming, increasingly urgent desire to see them gone or to go off and be by myself.

It is actually more than a desire. It is a real need, something absolutely essential to me. If I were forced to stay in company, and if I had to stay not so much listening as simply hearing the conversation of other people, I know that some kind of accident would happen to me. I'm not sure what exactly. Who knows, after all? I'd probably faint, I suppose, yes, that's it, I'd pass out!

I love my solitude so much that I cannot even bear to have others sleeping under the same roof as me. I could never live in Paris, for example. I die a slow death when I'm there. It's a kind of annihilation of the spirit for me; both my mind and my body are tortured by the consciousness of a vast, seething mass of humanity living around me there, awake or asleep. I tell you, other people's sleep is even more painful to me than their speech! I can never rest while I know, while I can feel behind that wall, say, the existence of others whose powers of reasoning are temporarily and regularly shut down.

Why am I like this? Who knows? Perhaps the reason is very simple. Maybe I just tire very quickly of anything that is not happening to myself. And there must be thousands like me. There are two kinds of people in the world. First there are those who need others and who are entertained, distracted, even soothed by company. Solitude for this kind of person is a huge, unremitting burden to bear, something as difficult and daunting as crossing a desert or climbing a dangerous glacier. Then there's the second type of person who gets tired, irritated and finally bored stiff in the company of others. For this kind of person, solitude is a balm, something they can lie back and bask in while their thoughts are allowed to roam free.

In other words we're talking about a perfectly normal psychological given. Some people are good at living extrovertly, others introvertly. I happen to be one of those whose capacity for attention to the outside world is very small and quickly exhausted. As soon as it reaches its limit I feel this intolerable unease throughout both my mind and my body.

As a result of this I have become, or rather had become, very attached to inanimate objects which were as important to me as human beings. My house has, or had, become a world in which I lived a solitary yet active life, surrounded by familiar objects, furniture and *bibelots* as lovable to me as human faces. Little by little I filled my house with these things and lived in their midst as happily as in the arms of a beloved woman whose warm, familiar embrace has become a prerequisite to a calm, untroubled existence.

I had had the house built within an attractive garden by which it was set back a little way from the road. It was situated on the outskirts of a town to which I could go whenever I felt like a little social life. All my servants lived in a building some way off at the end of a vegetable garden surrounded by a high wall. So beautifully soothing to me was the dark enfolding of the night in the silence of my secluded home, nestling as it did under the leaves of the huge surrounding trees, that every evening I used to put off going to bed the longer to savour it.

This particular night, they were putting on a production of *Sigurd* at the local theatre. It was the first time I had heard this beautiful, fairytale opera and I enjoyed it enormously. I was walking happily home, my ears full of the lovely arias, in my mind's eye seeing again the magical scenery. It was very, very dark indeed, so dark, in fact, that I could hardly see the road, and several times nearly fell into the ditch. From the tollgate to my house it's about a kilometre, maybe more – in other words, about a twenty-minute gentle walk. It was between one and half past one in the morning. The sky cleared a little above me and the sad old crescent moon of the last quarter appeared. The new crescent moon, the one which rises at about four or five in the afternoon, is bright and cheerful like polished silver but the one rising after midnight is a dismal, red-dish, rather gloomy one, a real Sabbath moon. Anybody with nocturnal habits will tell you that, I'm sure. The first, however slender, however threadlike, throws a shining brilliance that fills the heart with delight and casts sharp shadows on the earth. The last hardly sheds more than a dying glow and that so dull as to make hardly any shadow at all.

I could see in the distance the dense mass which was my garden when, out of nowhere, it seemed, a sort of unease began to creep over me at the thought of entering it. I slackened my pace. The air was balmy. The great clump of trees ahead looked like a tomb beneath which my house lay buried.

I opened my gate and began to walk up the long avenue of sycamores leading to the house, arched to make a vault-like tunnel, with banks of flowers on either side, then lawns where flowerbeds formed vague ovals among the pale shadows. As I approached the house, I was gripped by a strange feeling of foreboding. I stopped in my tracks. There was not a sound to be heard. Not a leaf rustled. What on earth was the matter with me, I wondered. I had been coming home like this for ten years with never a hint of any anxiety in my mind. I was not frightened. I have never been afraid of the night. Had I spotted some prowler or burglar, anger would have trans-lated itself into physical action and I would have hurled myself at him without the slightest hesitation. Besides, I was armed. I had my revolver on me. But I never touched it. I knew that I needed to control by myself the fear I could feel stirring into life within me.

What was it? Some premonition? The mysterious kind of premonition which grips a man's senses when they are about to witness something inexplicable? Perhaps so. Who knows? As I moved forward, my flesh began to creep. When I reached the outside walls of my vast house with its closed shutters I felt I needed to wait a few minutes before opening the front door and going in. I sat on a garden seat under my drawing room windows. Trembling a little, I leaned my head against the wall and focused on the shadowy bushes beyond. For the first few moments I noticed nothing unusual. I had a little roaring in the ears but I get that often. It's as if I can hear trains passing, bells ringing, or the stamp of a crowd on the march.

Soon, however, this roaring became more distinct, sharper in tone and more specific. I had been wrong in thinking this was the usual sound of blood coursing through my arteries. This was a very particular sound which, however difficult to define, was coming, there was no doubt about this now, from within my house itself.

Through the wall I could hear it continuously, more of a tremor than a noise, the vague shifting of a host of things, as if all the furniture were being picked up, shaken, then dragged quietly off. Well! As you can imagine, for a very long time I wondered whether I was hearing things. But having glued my ear to the shutter to try and find out what this disturbance inside my home was, I came to the firm conclusion that something incomprehensible and abnormal was going on. I was not so much frightened as . . . how can I put it? . . . terrified with astonishment. I did not load my revolver, guessing quite correctly, as it turned out, that there was no earthly reason to do so. I waited.

For a long time I continued to wait, not knowing what to do, with a mind perfectly clear though full of trepidation. By now I was standing listening to the noise increase at times to an ear-shattering pitch. At other times, too, this mysterious upheaval sounded like a growl of impatience or even of anger. Suddenly ashamed of being such a coward, I got hold of my bunch of keys, chose the one I needed, rammed it into the lock, turned it twice, then flung the door open with such force I sent it crashing against the interior wall.

It sounded like gunshot as the noise echoed from top to bottom of my entire house, from which came now a thunderous reverberation. It was so sudden and so deafening that I recoiled a few paces in horror. Although I knew it was still useless, this time I did take my revolver out of its holster.

Again, I waited for . . . I don't know how long . . . a little while I suppose. What I could now hear was the extraordinary sound of steps coming down the stairway and on to the parquet and the carpets – the sound not of shoes or of human footwear but the clatter of wooden and iron crutches clashing like cymbals, or so it seemed. Suddenly, what should I see waddling over the threshold of my own room but the big armchair in which I used to sit to read. It came out into the garden. Others from the drawing room followed it and were followed in turn by low settees crawling crocodile-like along on their squat little legs. All my other chairs leapt out like goats, with footstools lolloping alongside.

You can imagine what I felt like! I slid behind some shrubbery and remained crouching there watching the procession continue to pass by, for they were all leaving, one after the other, quickly or slowly, according to size and weight. My piano, my full-size grand piano galloped wildly past me with a musical murmur in its flank; the smallest objects such as hairbrushes and crystal chandelier droplets crawled like ants on the ground accompanied by glass goblets on which the moonlight cast little glow-worms of phosphorescence; curtains, hangings, tapestries spread like pools and stretched out octopus-like tentacles of fabric as they swam past. My desk hove into view, a rare eighteenth-century piece now containing some photographs and all the letters tracing the sad history of my painful love-life.

I suddenly lost my fear. I threw myself on it and held it down as if it had been a burglar or a woman attempting to flee. However, there was no stopping it and despite all my angry efforts I could not even slow down its inexorable progress. In my desperate struggle against this appalling power I was thrown to the ground, then rolled over and dragged along the gravel. In no time, the rest of the furniture in its train began to trample all over me, bruising my legs in the process. When I let go of the desk the rest of the pieces careered over my body as a cavalry charge mows down a fallen rider.

Frightened witless, I managed to drag myself away from the avenue and hide myself again behind the trees, from which position I watched everything down to the smallest, the most modest of my former possessions, including some of whose existence I was not even aware, all disappear.

Then in the distance, from within my home now echoing as empty houses do, I heard a tremendous noise of doors shutting. My house from attic to cellar rang with the sound of slamming until the door which I myself had just recently opened in terror finally also closed.

I too now fled and ran towards the town. I did not regain any degree of composure until I was again in the streets where late-night revellers were making their way home. I went to a hotel where I was known and rang the bell. I dusted myself down before going in to explain that I had lost my keys, among them the one for the garden gate where my servants slept in the separate house within the fence protecting my fruit and vegetables from thieves.

I dived into the bed they gave me and covered myself up to the eyes. I could not sleep, however, and as I lay waiting for daylight I could hear my heart pounding. I had ordered my servants to be alerted at dawn, and at seven o'clock my manservant came knocking at the door.

He looked devastated.

'Something dreadful happened in the night, Monsieur,' he said.

'Oh? What was that?'

'Monsieur has been robbed of every single article in the house, every single one, down to the very smallest piece.'

This news pleased me. I have no idea why. Who knows? I felt perfectly in control, certain that I could pretend and that I need tell no one what I had seen. I was sure I could keep this terrible secret hidden in my subconscious. I replied: 'It must be the same people who stole my keys. We must let the police know at once. I shall join you in a few minutes after I've got dressed.'

The inquiry lasted five months. Nothing was discovered. Not a single piece of mine was recovered and not the slightest trace of robbers ever found. My God! Imagine if I'd said what I knew! If I'd said a word about that, it would have been myself rather than any robbers who would have been locked up for believing such a thing! Oh yes, I kept my mouth shut all right! But I never refurnished the house. That would have been pointless. The whole business would have started up again. I wished never to return there. I stayed away therefore and never saw the place again.

I came and lived in a hotel in Paris where I consulted doctors about the state of my nerves which had been giving me a lot of trouble ever since that appalling night. They recommended that I do some travelling and I followed their advice.

II

I started with a trip to Italy, where the sun did me good. For six months I wandered about between Venice, Florence, Rome and Naples. Then I toured through Sicily admiring its wildlife and the monuments left by the Greeks and others. I went on to Africa and made a leisurely crossing of the great, calm, yellow desert. Here I saw camels roam, as well as gazelles and Arab vagabonds, and on its light, transparent air no trace of animosity ever seems to be felt, either by day or by night.

I returned to France via Marseille where, despite traditional Provençal gaiety, the relative diminution in light cast a tinge of sadness over me. Returning to this continent I felt strangely like an invalid who, though allegedly cured of his illness, knows from the dull ache that he feels that it is merely dormant within him.

Then I came back to Paris. After a month I was bored with it. It was autumn, and before winter set in I wanted to make a tour of Normandy, then still unfamiliar territory to me. I started in Rouen, of course, and for a week wandered around enthusiastically, finding fresh delights in the medieval city of Gothic monuments which is such an astonishing and wonderful museum in itself.

One afternoon at around four o'clock I turned in to an incredible street where a river called Eau de Robec flowed with water as black as ink. While I was looking with great interest at the bizarre architecture of the houses there, my attention was drawn to a series of antique shops set all in a row, one next door to the other. Those crooked old dealers in antiquity had certainly picked the right place. The street was eerie, with its pointed tile and slate roofs where ancient weather vanes still creaked on high. Stored in the dark interiors of these shops could be seen carved sideboards piled high, one on top of the other, Nevers pottery, Moustiers ware, painted statuettes, carved oak figures, crucifixes, Madonnas, saints, church ornaments, chasubles, copes and even one or two holy vases, as well as a tabernacle conveniently vacated by the Godhead. What amazing places they were, these huge, tall houses like Aladdin's caves crammed to bursting with all kinds of objects of seemingly finite use, but which had long survived their first owners and endured through their century, their times and fashions, to be bought as curiosities by the generations that followed!

My fondness for such things was revived in this enclave of the ancient. I went from shop to shop, crossing in two strides the little bridges made of four worm-eaten planks thrown across the evil-smelling Eau de Robec. God help me! What a frightful shock I was soon to get! On one side of a vault packed tightly with stuff and looking like the entrance to the catacombs of some furniture cemetery, what should appear before my eyes but one of my own most beautiful cupboards! I approached, trembling in every limb, so much so in fact that at first I dared not touch it. Tentatively I stretched out my hand. Yes, it was mine all right; a unique, Louis XIII piece, once seen never forgotten. Suddenly, peering into the darkest depths of this gallery I saw three of my armchairs covered in petit point, and farther on still, my two Henri II tables, such rare examples that people used to come from Paris to look at them.

Imagine! Just imagine what I felt like!

On I went nevertheless. Half-dead with fright, still I advanced. I'm brave, I'll say that for me! Nearly paralysed with dread by now, I inched forward like a knight from the dark ages making his way through the enchanted forest. As I moved on, with every step I gradually found everything that had once belonged to me – my chandeliers, my books, my pictures, my curtains, rugs, armour, everything except the desk full of love-letters, of which there was no sign anywhere.

Farther in still I went, descending into the deepest of the dark galleries below, then climbing up to the upper storeys. I was alone. I called but never an answer came. I was alone. There was no one else in the vast, winding labyrinth of a house. Night fell and, reluctant to leave, I sat down in the shadows on one of the chairs formerly my own. From time to time I shouted, 'Hallo! Hallo! Anybody there?'

I must have been there for more than an hour when I heard footsteps; soft, slow footsteps coming from I knew not where. I nearly ran away but, bracing myself, I called out once more and noticed a gleam of light coming from the next room.

'Who's there?' called a voice.

'A customer,' I replied.

'Don't you think it's a bit late to just wander into somebody's shop like this?'

'I've been waiting over an hour to see you,' I went on.

'You could have come back tomorrow.'

'I shall have left Rouen tomorrow.'

I dared not go forward and he showed no sign of coming to me. I could still see the gleam of light shining on a tapestry which showed two angels flying over a battlefield. That was mine also.

'Well? Are you coming or not?' I said.

'I'm waiting for you,' he replied.

I rose and went in his direction.

Standing in the middle of a large room was a very small man, phenomenally fat, and extremely ugly. He had a meagre, ill-trimmed, yellowing beard and not a hair on his head. Not one! As he held up a candle in his outstretched hand to look me over, his skull seemed to me like a little moon in this enormous room filled with old furniture. In his puffy face there were deep furrows into which the eyes disappeared. I haggled over three of my own chairs and, giving my room number at the hotel, paid a vast sum of money for them. They were to be delivered the following morning at nine o'clock. I then left the room and with much ceremony he saw me to the door.

I made straight for the house of the central commissioner of police whom I told about the theft of my furniture and my recent rediscovery of it. He wired forthwith, requesting information from the office of the public prosecutor who originally investigated the theft, and asked me to wait till the reply came. An hour later, to my great satisfaction, he was in possession of the necessary information.

'I intend to arrest this man,' he said. 'His suspicions may have been aroused and he may try to spirit away your property. Would you like to go and have your dinner, then come back to me in two hours' time? I shall have him here by then and will question him further in your presence.'

'Most willingly, Monsieur. I'm very grateful indeed to you.'

I went and dined at my hotel, eating more heartily than I could have imagined possible, very largely I suppose because I was so glad at the prospect of the man soon being under arrest. Two hours later I returned to the police officer's house where he was waiting for me.

'Well, Monsieur,' he said, as soon as he saw me, 'we

didn't manage to find your man. My officers have been unable to get hold of him.'

Oh no! I felt faint.

'But . . . you found the house, didn't you?'

'Easily. It will be under surveillance and guarded till he returns. As for the man himself, he's disappeared.'

'Disappeared?'

'Disappeared. Normally he spends the evening with his neighbour, another dealer, a real old witch, the widow Bidouin. She hasn't seen him tonight and can give us no information concerning his whereabouts. We shall have to wait until morning.'

I left him. How sinister and how haunted did the streets of Rouen seem to me then. I hardly slept all night. Each time I nodded off it was into one nightmare after another. I did not wish to appear too anxious or impatient, so waited until ten o'clock the following morning before making my way to the police. The dealer had not reappeared. His shop remained closed. The commissioner said to me: 'I've gone through all the necessary procedures. The public prosecutor's office is aware of these developments. We shall make our way together to the store and have it opened up. You will show me all the items of property which are yours.'

We were whisked away in a coupé. Police officers with a locksmith in attendance were stationed at the shop entrance door which was now open. Upon entering I saw no sign of my cupboard, my armchairs, my tables, or any single one of the objects with which my house had been furnished, nothing at all – whereas the previous evening I had been unable to take a step without bumping into one or other of my former possessions.

The commissioner was surprised. At first he looked at me with suspicion.

'My God, Monsieur!' I said to him, 'isn't it a bit of a coincidence that my property should disappear at precisely the same time as the dealer?'

He smiled.

'True enough! It was a mistake to buy your own things yesterday and pay for them. It's obviously tipped him off.'

I went on: 'What I simply cannot understand is that all the space taken up by my furniture is now filled completely with other stuff.'

'Oh!' replied the commissioner, 'he's had all night . . . and used accomplices, no doubt. This house is bound to lead in some way into the one next door. But don't worry, Monsieur, leave it all to me. The devil won't escape us for long, not while we're sitting on top of his lair, at least.'

Oh my heart, my poor heart! How wildly it was beating!

I stayed for about two weeks in Rouen. The man never returned. My God! My God! Who in the world would ever be able to get in *his* way? Take *him* by surprise? On the morning of my sixteenth day there I received from my gardener, whom I had left in charge of the looted and still deserted house, the following strange letter:

Monsieur,

May I inform Monsieur that last night something occurred here that no one, not even the police, can account for. All the furniture has come back; all, without exception and down to the smallest article. The house is now exactly as it was on the day before the robbery. We cannot get our heads around it. It happened between Friday night and the early hours of Saturday morning. The paths are all trampled over as though everything had been dragged from the gate to the front door. It was the same in reverse on the day we found them to have disappeared.

We await instructions from Monsieur whose humble servant I remain, Raudin, Philippe.

Oh no! No! No! No! I will not go back!
I took the letter to the commissioner of Rouen.
'A clever little restitution,' he said. 'Let's play dead. We'll pick him up one of these days.'
But he's never been picked up. No, they've never managed to pick him up and now I'm as terrified of him as if I had a wild beast on my tracks. Nowhere to be found! He is nowhere to be found, that monster with the moon-skull! They'll never catch him!
He'll never go back to that place of his! What does he

care about it? *I'm* the only one who can catch him and I won't do it!

I won't! I won't! I won't!

And even if he does go back, even if he does return to his shop, who could prove that my furniture was there? There's only my word to go on and I can tell that's not being seen as entirely reliable these days. Oh, no! I could no longer go on living that way. I could no longer keep secret what I had seen. I could not carry on living as normal with the fear at the back of my mind that something like that could start up again. I came to see the director of this clinic and told him everything. After a lengthy consultation, he said: 'Would you be willing, Monsieur, to come and live with us here for a while?'

'More than willing, Monsieur.'

'Do you have money?'

'Yes, Monsieur.'

'Would you like a private room?'

'Yes, Monsieur.'

'Would you like to have friends come and see you?'

'No, Monsieur, no one. The man in Rouen might want to get his own back and follow me here.'

And so I have been alone, quite alone, for three months now. I'm more or less happy. Only one thing worries me: what if the dealer went mad? What if he were brought to this clinic? You see? Even in prison you're never absolutely safe you know!

The Horla

Doctor Marrande, one of the most eminent psychiatrists in the country, had invited three of his colleagues and four others in the field of the natural sciences to spend an hour at his clinic considering the case of one of his patients. When they were all gathered, he said to them: 'I should like to present to you the strangest and most disturbing case I have ever come across. I shall say nothing ahead of time about this patient, but let him speak for himself.'

The doctor rang and a man entered, accompanied by a member of staff. He was extremely thin, cadaverous even, as some madmen look when they are consumed by an obsession. Their bodies seem ravaged by one sick thought which devours them faster than any disease or consumption. Having greeted the company and sat down, the man spoke.

'Gentlemen, I am well aware of what brings you here. I am happy to comply with Dr Marrande's request for me to give you my history. For a long time he himself believed I was mad. Today he is not so sure. Some time in the near future you will realize that, unfortunately, not only for myself but for you and all the rest of humanity, my mind is as healthy, clear and as lucid as your own. Let me first of all give you the facts.

I am forty-two years old and unmarried. My income is sufficient for me to live a fairly luxurious kind of life. I live in a property which I own on the banks of the Seine at Biessard, near Rouen. I like hunting and I like fishing. Beyond the rocky hillsides behind my house lies one of the most beautiful forests in the whole of France, the forest of Roumare. And in front of the house, which is very large and very old, lies one of the most beautiful rivers in the world. Moreover, the house itself is attractive: it is painted white and stands in the middle of parkland which extends as far as the rocky hillsides I mentioned earlier.

My staff consists, or rather consisted, of a coachman, a gardener, a manservant, a cook and a laundry-cum-scullery maid. All these people had lived there with me for between ten and sixteen years. They were long familiar with my ways, with the running of the house, with the neighbourhood, everything. They made an excellent, harmonious team, a point which it is important to bear in mind in what follows.

I should add that since the Seine, as you probably know, is navigable as far as Rouen, on the stretch of it in front of my house I used to see daily all kinds of sea-going vessels from all over the world pass up and down stream, some under sail, some under steam.

Well, about a year last autumn, I suddenly began to suffer inexplicable spells of a strange malaise. To begin with, I was prey to a kind of nervous anxiety which kept me awake for entire nights at a stretch, a kind of hyper-sensitivity which made me jump at the least little sound. I began to have periods of moodiness and sudden fits of anger for no apparent reason. I consulted a doctor who prescribed cold showers and potassium bromide.

I followed his advice and took a shower morning and evening, as well as the bromide. Quite soon I did in fact manage to start sleeping again, but this time sleep turned out to be even more intolerable than the insomnia. As soon as my head hit the pillow, my eyes closed and I was out. I mean out completely. I fell into absolute nothing-ness, a void, a total blank. My self became completely dead until I was suddenly, horribly awoken by the most appalling sensation. An unbearable weight was lying on my chest and another mouth was sucking the life out of me through my own. I shall never forget the terrible shock of it! Just imagine a man asleep and in the process of being murdered. He wakes with the knife in his throat. He can hear his own death-rattle, feel his own blood ooze out of him. He cannot breathe. He knows he is going to die but not why – that's exactly what it felt like!

I was losing a dangerous amount of weight all the time and suddenly realized that my coachman, a big, solid sort of fellow, was doing the same thing. I said to him in the end, 'Look, Jean, there's definitely something wrong with you. What d'you think is the matter?' 'To tell you the truth, monsieur,' he said, 'I think I've caught whatever you've got. My nights seem to be eating into my days.' I began to think that there was something noxious permeating the house, something poisonous, maybe, emanating from the river.

I had decided to spend two or three months away, despite the fact that the hunting season was in full swing, when something strange happened. I might easily have missed it, so trivial did it at first seem but it led to a series of such unbelievable, fantastical events that I decided after all, to stay.

One night, being thirsty, I drank half a glass of water and noticed when I did so that the carafe on my bedside table had been full up as far as its glass stopper. During the night I had one of those terrible awakenings I just mentioned. Still shaking, I lit my candle and was about to take another drink of water when I noticed to my stupefaction that the carafe was now empty. I could not believe my eyes. Either someone had come into the room or I was acting unconsciously in my sleep.

The following night I wanted to see if the same thing would happen. This time I locked my door to make sure no one could come into the room. I went to sleep and woke up as I did every night. *Someone* had drunk all the water I had seen there with my own eyes only two hours before. But *who*? Myself, obviously, and yet I could have almost sworn that I had made no movement in my deep and painful sleep.

I resorted to various stratagems in order to convince myself that I was not doing these things unconsciously. One night I put next to the carafe a bottle of vintage claret as well as a glass of milk, which I hate, and a piece of chocolate cake, which I love. Both the wine and the cake remained intact. But the water and the milk disappeared. None of the solid foodstuffs had had inroads made in them, only the liquids – the water and milk especially.

I was still in agonizing doubt. Maybe it was still I myself who was getting up without any consciousness of it. Maybe it was I who even drank the liquids I detested. My senses could have been so drugged that in sleep they were completely altered. In that state it was possible for me to have shed my former dislikes and acquired new tastes altogether.

I tried another way to catch myself out. I wrapped everything which was likely to be touched in thin muslin, which in turn I covered with the finest linen napkins. Then, just before getting into bed, I rubbed my face, hands and moustache all over with black lead. When I awoke, the materials were still spotless. They had, however, been moved. The napkins lay differently from the way I had placed them, and, more importantly, both the water and the milk had been drained off. This time my door had been locked with an extra security key, the shutters had been padlocked also just in case, and no one therefore could possibly have come into the room. So I had to ask myself the terrifying question of who it was that was in there with me every night.

I see you smile, gentlemen. You have already decided that I am mad, I can see. I have rushed you somewhat. I should have described in greater detail the feelings of a man with a completely clear mind, safe inside his own house, seeing water disappear from his carafe while he's asleep. I should have conveyed to you better the kind of torture I experienced every morning and every evening. I should have described how annihilating the sleep was and how hideous the awakening. But let me continue.

Quite suddenly, these inexplicable occurrences ceased. Nothing was touched in my room. It was over. I began to feel much better in myself. I felt a sense of relief return, particularly when I learned that Monsieur Legite, one of my neighbours, was showing many of my own earlier symptoms. Once more I was sure it must have something to do with our location and that it was something in the atmosphere. My coachman, incidentally, had become extremely ill and had stopped working for me a month earlier.

Winter had passed and it was now early spring. One day I was walking near one of my rose-borders when I saw, I tell you I saw with my very own eyes and right next to me at that, the stalk of one of the most beautiful roses break off exactly as though an invisible hand had plucked it. The flower described the curve which an invisible arm would have made to bring it to someone's face, then hung terrifyingly suspended in mid-air all by itself, no more than three feet away from my eyes. Scared witless, I lunged forward to grab it. Nothing! Gone! I suddenly became furious with myself. No man in his right mind could have hallucinations like that! But was that what it was? I looked for the stem of the rose again and found straight away where it had been broken off between two other blooms on the same branch. I knew there had been three earlier on. I had seen them.

I went indoors, shaken to the core. I assure you, gentlemen, I am quite clear about this. I do not now and never have believed in the supernatural. But from that moment onwards, I knew as surely as I know night follows day that somewhere near me was an invisible being. It had haunted me before, left me for a while and was now back.

A short while later I had proof.

My staff began to quarrel among themselves every day. It was always over seemingly trivial matters, but for me they were full of significance. One day one of my best glasses, a beautiful Venetian piece, fell for no apparent reason from the dining room dresser and smashed into smithereens. My manservant blamed the maid who in turn blamed somebody else, and so it continued. Doors firmly locked in the evening were found next day wide open. Every night milk was stolen from the pantry . . .

and so on and so forth ad nauseam. What was all this about? What on earth was happening? I vacillated, terrified, torn between wanting to know and dreading what I might learn. Once again the house returned to normal and once more I began to think I must have dreamed the whole thing, until the following events occurred.

It was nine o'clock on the evening of 20 July and very warm. I had left my window open wide and light from a lamp on my table fell on a volume of Musset open at *Nuit de Mai*. I myself was stretched out on a sofa and had nodded off. After about forty minutes or so, awakened by a strange sort of feeling, I opened my eyes again but kept perfectly still. At first nothing happened. Then, as I watched, one of the pages of the book turned over, seemingly by itself. Not a breath of air had wafted through the window. Puzzled, I waited and in another four minutes or so I saw, I saw with my own eyes, gentlemen, another page rise and place itself over the first, exactly as if turned by invisible fingers. The armchair next to it seemed unoccupied but I knew perfectly well *it* was there. I leapt across the room to grab it, touch it, to seize hold of it somehow or other. But before I reached it, the chair, seemingly of its own accord, turned over backwards as if fleeing from me. The lamp also fell and went out, its glass smashed. The window was suddenly flung back against its hinges as if by some intruder making his escape . . . oh, my God! I rang the bell furiously and when my manservant came, said, 'I've knocked all this stuff over and smashed it. Go and fetch another lamp will you?'

I slept no more that night. Yet I could still have made some sort of mistake. When you wake from a snooze you're always a little bit befuddled. Could it have been I who turned the armchair over and upset the lamp, rushing about like a mad thing? No! Of course it was not! I had not the slightest doubt about that. Yet that was what I wanted to believe.

Now. What should I call this . . . Being? The Invisible One? No, that would not do. I decided to call it the Horla. Don't ask me why. So I was going to be stuck with this Horla indefinitely. Night and day I could feel it there. I knew it was close to me the whole time, yet totally elusive. I also knew for certain that with each passing hour, each passing minute, even, it was drawing the life out of me. I was driven to distraction by the fact that I could never see it. I lit every lamp in the house. Maybe given proper illumination it could be exposed.

Then, finally, I saw it. Believe it or not, I saw it.

I was sitting with some book or other in front of me, not really reading. With every nerve on edge, I was waiting and watching for this being I could feel near me. I knew it was somewhere. But where? What was it doing? How could I get hold of it? Opposite was my bed, an old oak four-poster. To my right was the fireplace. On the left the door, which I had made sure was locked. Behind me was a very large, mirrored wardrobe before which I shaved and dressed every day. Whenever I passed it I could see myself full length. So there I was, pretending to this presence which I knew was spying on me that I was reading. All of a sudden I felt it reading over my shoulder, brushing against my ear. Leaping to my feet, I turned round so quickly that I nearly fell over. Believe it or not, though the room was bright as day, there was no sign of me in the mirror. It was empty, clear and full of light. But my reflection was not in it, despite the fact that I was standing directly in front of it. I looked at the large glass, clear now from top to bottom. I looked at it in terror. I dared not take a step forward, knowing that this being was in between. I knew that although it would slip away from me again, its own invisible body had absorbed my own reflection. I was so frightened! Then suddenly I saw myself begin to appear from the misty depths of the mirror, rising as if from a body of water. The water itself seemed to shift slowly from left to right revealing, second by second, an increasingly sharper reflection of myself. It was like the end of an eclipse. What was concealing me looked like an opaqueness gradually turning transparent. Finally I could see myself clearly again, as I do when I look in the mirror every day. But now I had seen it. The terror of that moment remains with me and makes me tremble still. The following day I came here and asked to be admitted.

And now, gentlemen, I come to the end of my story. Having been fairly sceptical for some time, Dr Marrande decided to make a little unaccompanied trip to my part of the world. It transpires that three of my neighbours are now in a similar condition to the one I have described, isn't that so?'

'Absolutely true!' the doctor replied.

'You instructed them to leave out some milk or water in the bedroom every night to see if these liquids disappeared or not. They did. They disappeared just as they did in my house, didn't they?'

With great seriousness the doctor replied, 'They did indeed.'

'So, gentlemen, a Being, some new Being which, like ourselves, will undoubtedly multiply and increase, is now on earth. What? Why are you smiling? Because the Being is still invisible? But, gentlemen, what a primitive organ is the eye! It can barely spot our basic needs for survival. It misses the infinitesimal as well as the infinite. It does not perceive the millions of tiny organisms present in a drop of water. It does not perceive the inhabitants, the plants and the earth of the planets closest to us; it does not apprehend what is transparent. Put it in front of a piece of non-reflecting glass and it fails to notice. We go careering straight into it as a bird trapped inside a house will continue to beat its skull against the window panes. It fails to perceive solid but transparent objects. Yet these things exist. It cannot see air which is essential to human life; wind, which is the most powerful force in nature, capable of lifting men off their feet, flattening buildings, uprooting trees, and raising the sea into mountains of water which pulverize cliffs of solid granite. Why should we be surprised if it cannot make out a new kind of body to the human, and different from it only in that it does not emit light. Do you see electricity? Yet of course it exists. What is this being, gentlemen? I believe it is what the earth is waiting for, to supersede humanity, to usurp our throne, to overwhelm and perhaps feed on us as we feed now on cattle and wild boar. We have sensed and dreaded it for centuries. We have heard its approach with terror. Our forefathers have been haunted forever by the Invisible.

It has come.

All the legends of spirits, hobgoblins and evil, elusive riders in the sky were about it. It is his arrival which man has been dreading with such trepidation. And you yourselves, gentlemen, all the activities you have been engaged in in the last few years – hypnotism, the power of suggestion, magnetism – all point towards the Invisible. And I tell you he is here. He roams about anxiously, just as primitive man did, ignorant as yet of his full power and potential which will be realized soon enough! Finally, gentlemen, here is an excerpt from a newspaper article which I have come across, published in Rio de Janeiro:

> An epidemic of apparent insanity appears to have been raging for some time in the province of São Paulo. The inhabitants of several villages have fled their homes and

abandoned their crops in the belief that they are being hunted and eaten by invisible vampires living off their sleeping breath and drinking nothing but water or occasionally milk.

I should add that a few days before my own first attack of the disease which nearly killed me, I distinctly remember having seen a three-master pass, flying the flag of Brazil . . . I told you that my house is situated near the river bank . . . No doubt he was hidden somewhere aboard that ship. That's all I have to say, gentlemen.'

Dr Marrande rose to his feet and murmured, 'I am in as much of a quandary as you all. I cannot tell if this man is mad or whether we both are . . . or whether . . . man's successor is already in our midst . . .'

Boule de Suif

For several days in succession remnants of the routed army had been passing through the town. Formerly disciplined units had now turned into a disorganized rabble and separated from their regiments and colours, men with dirty, unkempt beards and uniforms in tatters now dragged their feet listlessly on. All the men looked crushed and exhausted, incapable of thought or resolve, marching out of sheer habit and collapsing with fatigue whenever they came to a halt. Bent under the weight of their rifles, they consisted mostly of reservists who until call-up were easy-going men used to minding their own business. These were combined with fit young conscripts, easily excited, easily scared and prone in equal measure to fight or flight. Mixed in with the latter and quickly identifiable by their red breeches were a few regulars, the remains of some division pulverized in battle, some sombrely uniformed gunners and a sprinkling of infantrymen of various sorts. The occasional glint of a helmet flashed as a dragoon lumbered clumsily in the steps of lighter soldiers of the line. Detachments of *francs-tireurs* also passed through, their bandit-like appearance contrasting vividly with their grandiose names: 'Avengers of Defeat', 'Citizens of the Tomb', 'Brothers to the Death'. Their leaders were former drapers, corn-merchants, soap- and tallow-dealers, turned soldiers by force of circumstance and officers on the strength of a fat wallet or a long moustache. Armed to the teeth and covered in gold-braided flannel, in loud, boastful voices they discussed plans of campaign as if the burden of the dying homeland rested on their broad shoulders alone. In fact, however, they often went in fear of their own men who, though brave in the extreme, were often criminal characters to whom rape and pillage were second nature.

Rumour had it that the Prussians were on the point of entering Rouen. The National Guard who for the previous two months had been carefully reconnoitring the nearby woods, sometimes shooting their own sentries in the process and preparing for action whenever a rabbit stirred in the bushes, had now returned to their firesides. With them, the arms, the uniforms and the entire military apparatus, which had made them the terror of the highroads for miles around, had all suddenly disappeared for good.

The last remaining French soldiers had finally crossed the Seine to reach Pont-Audemer via Saint-Sever and Bourg-Achard. In the rear, flanked by two staff-officers, their despairing general walked. Incapable of commanding this undisciplined mob, he was bewildered by the disarray in which his normally victorious nation now found itself and, despite the legendary courage shown, by the disastrous scale of its defeat.

A deep quiet, an atmosphere of silent, terrified foreboding hung over the city. Many of its inhabitants, fat and flabby businessmen waiting anxiously for the conquerors to come, trembled with fear lest the roasting spits and long kitchen knives of their comfortable homes be taken for weapons. Life seemed to have ground to a halt. Shops were closed and streets deserted. From time to time a stealthy figure slithered by, frightened by the silence, and keeping close to the shadows of the walls.

The strain of waiting made everyone long for the enemy to arrive.

On the afternoon following the departure of the French troops, a few Uhlans appeared out of the blue and galloped through the town. A short while later, a dark mass of troops swept down the hill of Sainte-Catherine as two further waves of invasion flooded the approaches from Darnetal and Boisguillaume. The advance guard of the three corps, arriving simultaneously, linked up on the Place de I'Hôtel de Ville. Along all the neighbouring streets, German troops poured, making the cobblestones ring with the heavy, measured stamp of their battalions.

Orders shouted in a foreign, gutteral tongue echoed between the walls of the houses, which appeared dead and deserted. Behind closed shutters many eyes watched the victors. The latter, according to the rules of war, were now masters both of the city and of the lives and fortunes of its denizens. These, in their darkened rooms, had fallen victim to the panic engendered by natural disasters, those devastating upheavals of the earth against which neither wisdom nor strength is of any avail. For the same feeling re-emerges each time the established order of things is upset, when security is destroyed and when everything protected by the laws of man or of nature finds itself at the mercy of some brutal, unreasoning force. The earthquake which crushes an entire population under the rubble of its houses; the river in swollen spate sweeping away the corpses of drowned peasants along with the bodies of their cattle and the rafters torn from their roofs; the glorious army which slaughters all who resist, takes others prisoner, pillaging by right of the sword, praising God to the roar of cannon; all of these are so many terrifying scourges which destroy our belief in eternal justice and any trust we may have been taught to place in divine protection or the power of human reason.

Small detachments of men were soon knocking on the door of every house and disappearing within. The time had come for the vanquished to show courtesy to the conquerors. After a short while, once their initial terror had loosened its grip, a new sort of calm descended. In many homes, a Prussian officer ate with the family. Sometimes he was sufficiently civil as to express polite sympathy with France, and distaste for his own part in the war. This sentiment was gratefully accepted by his hosts and, besides, who knew when they would be glad of his protection? If they handled matters diplomatically with him, perhaps not so many men would be billeted on them. Why offend someone who had complete power over you? Such an attitude would smack more of temerity than courage, and temerity was no longer one of the failings of the burghers of Rouen as it had been in the days when the heroic defence of their town had brought them both honour and glory. Lastly, they found their greatest justification in traditional French urbanity: it was perfectly permissible to act politely to the foreign soldier in your own home provided you demonstrated little friendliness toward him in public. Outside they were strangers, but in the house you and he could chat away together as long as you liked. The German would stay on with the family a little longer each evening, basking in the warmth of his new home from home.

The town itself gradually began to reassume its normal appearance. Though the French were slow to re-emerge, the streets swarmed with Prussian soldiers. And indeed, it had to be said, these Blue Hussars arrogantly trailing their instruments of death along the pavements were no more contemptuous of ordinary civilians than the French Light Infantry who had sat drinking in exactly the same cafés no more than a year before.

Nevertheless, there was something in the air, some strangeness hard to pin down, an unbearably alien atmosphere which hung about like a smell. It was the feel of

Occupation. It permeated homes as well as public places, altered the taste of things and made people feel they were living in some foreign land surrounded by dangerous tribes of barbarians.

The conquerors demanded money and lots of it at that. The rich inhabitants kept paying up as of course they could afford to do. But the more a Norman businessman's wealth grows, the more keenly does he feel any sacrifice of it, and the more he suffers to see his fortune pass into the hands of another.

Meanwhile, five or six miles downstream, towards Croisset, Dieppedalle or Biessart, bargees and fishermen often hauled up the bodies of German soldiers bloated under their uniforms, stabbed or kicked to death, thrown over a parapet into the water, their heads smashed in with a stone. All the secret acts of vengeance, the brutal yet understandable deeds of quiet heroism, the silent attacks more dangerous than pitched battle and less glorious in consequence, all slid downwards into the bed of the river. For hatred of the Stranger will always arm the intrepid few ready to give up their lives for their principles.

At length, since the invaders, while imposing a rule of iron upon the town, had not committed any of the atrocities which rumour had attributed to them throughout the course of their triumphal progress, confidence began to return to the populace and the desire to conduct business stirred again in the hearts of the local tradesmen. Some of them had major commercial interests in Le Havre, still in the hands of the French. They were keen therefore to try and reach that port overland via Dieppe and thence by ship. Using the influence of the German officers whom they had come to know, they managed to secure a transport permit from the general in command.

Accordingly, a large, four-horse coach was hired for the journey. Ten people reserved places on board and it was decided to meet one Tuesday morning before daybreak so as not to attract attention. For some time now the ground had been frozen hard, and on the Monday, at about three in the afternoon, great dark clouds from the north brought snow which fell continuously all that evening and throughout the night.

At half past four in the morning, the travellers met in the courtyard of the Hôtel de Normandie where they were to board the coach. They were still half-asleep and shivering with cold under their wraps. It was hard for them to make each other out in the dark, and with so much heavy winter clothing on they all looked like portly priests in long cassocks. Two of the men, however, recognized each other; a third joined them and the trio stood chatting.

'I'm taking my wife out of this,' said one.

'So am I.'

'Me too.'

The first man added: 'We won't be coming back to Rouen in a hurry, and if the Prussians advance on Le Havre, we'll be taking off for England.'

Being like-minded fellows, all three had made similar

plans for the future. Still there was no sign of the horses. Every so often a small lantern carried by an ostler appeared in one dark doorway only to disappear into another. The sound came occasionally of horses' hooves stamping on the ground, muffled by the dung in the stalls. From the far end of the building the voice of a man swearing at the animals could also be heard. A faint tinkling of bells indicated that the harness was being put on and this sound was soon transformed into a continuous jingle, changing rhythm with the horse's movements, stopping occasionally and then starting up again with a sudden jerk and the dull thud of an iron-shod hoof hitting the ground. Suddenly the door closed. Silence fell. The frozen townsfolk stopped talking and stood there, stiff and motionless.

A curtain of white flakes swirled ceaselessly to the ground, blurring outlines and powdering every object with a dusting of ice. In the deep silence of the town buried in wintry stillness nothing could be heard save the vague, mysterious rustling whisper, more sensation than sound, of the falling snow, a mingling of weightless particles which seemed to be filling the sky and covering the world.

The man reappeared with his lantern, leading at the end of a rope a miserable and unwilling horse. He tethered it to the hitching post and fastened the traces, spending a long time fixing the harness with one hand while the other held the lantern. As he was about to fetch the second horse, he noticed the travellers standing motionless and already white with snow from head to toe.

'Why don't you get on board?' he said. 'At least you'll be under cover.'

This thought had apparently not occurred to them before and they rushed to the coach. The three men settled their wives at the far end then got in beside them. The other indistinct, muffled figures took the remaining places in silence.

Their feet sank into the straw covering the floor. The ladies at the far end, having brought little copper foot-warmers which ran on chemical fuel, now began lighting these contraptions. For some time they could be heard quietly extolling the virtues of them and exchanging civilities.

At last the coach was ready, with six rather than four horses harnessed because of the heavy weather. A voice from outside called: 'Everybody in?' They set off.

The coach lumbered slowly and laboriously forward. The wheels sank into the snow, the whole vehicle creaked and groaned, the horses slipped and panted and steamed and the driver's huge whip cracked ceaselessly. It darted in every direction, knotting then uncoiling itself like a thin snake to give a sudden sting to a firm rump which then tensed into greater effort.

Imperceptibly it grew lighter. The feathery snowflakes, likened by one of the passengers – a Rouen man born and bred – to a fall of cotton-wool, had stopped. A murky light filtered through vast, lowering clouds whose leaden tints set off the dazzling whiteness of the countryside. Against it stood out here a row of tall trees covered with frost, there a cottage in a cowl of snow. Inside the coach, by the melancholy light of dawn, the travellers began to cast inquisitive glances at each other. At the far end, in the best places, Monsieur and Madame Loiseau, whole-sale wine merchants of the rue Grand Point sat dozing opposite each other. Once clerk to another wine merchant, he had bought his master's business when the latter went bankrupt, and made a fortune. He sold at a very low price very poor wine to small country retailers and was considered by his friends and acquaintances to be a wily old rascal with the typical Norman mixture of hearti-ness and guile in his blood. His reputation as a crook was so well established that one evening, at the Prefecture, Monsieur Tournel, a songwriter and raconteur of locally legendary dry and caustic wit, had suggested to the ladies, who were looking, as he thought, a little drowsy, that they should get up a game of *l'oiseau vole*. The joke spread like wildfire through the Prefect's drawing rooms and from there to others of the town, having the whole province in stitches for a good month.

Loiseau himself had a reputation moreover for prac-tical jokes in both good and dubious taste and whenever his name came up in conversation, someone would be sure to say, 'Priceless, old Loiseau.' He was a small man with a large paunch and a ruddy face framed by grizzled sidewhiskers. His wife, tall, stout and determined looking, had a shrill voice and a brisk manner. It was she who ran the shop and did the book-keeping while he kept business bubbling with his lively bonhomie.

Next to them, more dignified, as might be expected from a member of a superior class, sat Monsieur Carré-Lamadon, a man of considerable substance, well established in the cotton trade, proprietor of three spinning-mills, officer of the *Légion d'honneur* and member of the General Council. Throughout the Empire he had remained leader of the loyal opposition solely in order to obtain a higher price for his support of a policy he had opposed with what he termed the weapons of a gentleman. Madame Carré-Lamadon, who was much younger than her husband, had been a source of constant comfort to all officers of good families who found themselves stationed at Rouen. This dainty, demure, pretty little thing sat swathed in furs opposite her husband and looked disconsolately round at the miserable interior of the coach.

Her neighbours, the Comte and the Comtesse Hubert de Bréville, were descended from one of the most ancient and noble families of Normandy. The Comte, an elderly gentleman of distinguished countenance and bearing, tried as hard as possible to accentuate through dress the resemblance he bore to Henri IV. The latter, according to proud family legend, had fathered a child on a Madame de Bréville whose husband had been rewarded with the title of Comte and the governorship of a province. A colleague of Monsieur Carré-Lamadon on the General Council, Comte Hubert was the Departmental representative of the Orleanists. The story of his marriage to the daughter of a small Nantes shipowner remained shrouded in mystery. But since the Comtesse was possessed of a distinguished manner and was said to have been the mistress of one of Louis-Philippe's sons, she was celebrated by the local aristocracy and her salon, the only one in which the spirit of genuine French chivalry still survived, was considered the most exclusive of the region. The Brévilles' fortune, all in landed property, was said to produce an annual income of half a million francs.

These six people occupied the far end of the coach and represented the wealthy, highly self-confident and stable element of society; respectable and morally upright men and women with a proper respect for both religion and principles. By strange coincidence, all the ladies happened to be seated on the same side. Next to the Comtesse were two nuns, telling their rosaries and muttering paternosters and aves. One was elderly with a face as pockmarked as if it had received a charge of grapeshot at point-blank range. The other, puny and sickly-looking about the face, had the narrow chest of the consumptive but appeared eaten up instead by the all-devouring faith of the visionary or martyr.

All eyes were now upon the man and woman sitting opposite the two nuns.

The man, Cornudet, was a well-known local democrat and the terror of all respectable people. For the previous twenty years he had been dipping his red whiskers into the tankards of every pro-democrat café around and with the help of friends and comrades had squandered the sizeable fortune left to him by his father, a retired confectioner. He waited impatiently for the coming of the Republic which would put him at last in the official position so many revolutionary libations had surely earned him. On the fabled Fourth of September, possibly as the result of a practical joke, he had been appointed Prefect. However, when he attempted to take up his duties, the Prefecture office boys left in sole charge of the place refused to acknowledge his authority and he had had to beat a retreat. He was a good-natured sort, harmless and willing, and had applied himself with commendable enthusiasm to the organization of the town's defences. He had had pits dug in the open country, all the saplings of the neighbouring forests felled and all the roads booby-trapped. Satisfied that he had done all he could, as the enemy advanced ever closer he had quickly retreated into town. Now, he thought, he could make himself so much more useful at Le Havre where defensive positions would also have to be put into place.

The woman, one of those usually known as a good-time girl, was famous for the premature portliness which had earned her the nickname Boule de Suif. Small, round as a barrel, fat as butter and with fingers tightly jointed like strings of small sausages, her glowing skin and the enormous bosom which strained under the constraints of her dress – as well as her freshness, which was a delight to the eye – made her hugely desirable and much sought after. She had a rosy apple of a face, a peony bud about to burst into bloom. Out of it looked two magnificent dark eyes shaded by thick black lashes. Further down was a charming little mouth complete with invitingly moist lips and tiny, gleaming pearly-white teeth. She was said to possess a variety of other inestimable qualities.

As soon as she was recognized there was frantic whispering among the respectable women, and the words 'prostitute' and 'public disgrace' were whispered loudly enough for her to raise her eyes. Her gaze as she met those of her neighbours was so direct and challenging that they all immediately fell silent. Everyone looked down again apart from Loiseau who watched her with a lecherous eye. Soon, however, conversation resumed between the three ladies whom the presence of this prostitute had made friends, and close ones at that. It seemed to them it was their duty to present a united front of marital dignity in the face of this shameless harlot. Institutionalized love always looks down on her more liberal sister.

The three men were also drawn together by the presence of Cornudet. Speaking in disparaging tones about the ever-present poor, they began to discuss money. Comte Hubert mentioned both the damage the Prussians had caused him and his losses as a result of stolen cattle and ruined crops, but in the confident tones of a great landowner, a millionaire ten times over who would recoup these losses within a year at most. Monsieur Carré-Lamadon, whose cotton business had been hard hit, had taken the precaution of sending 600,000 francs to England so as to have, as usual, something stored away for a rainy day. As for Loiseau, he had managed to sell the French Commissariat all the *vin ordinaire* he had left in his cellars so that it now owed him a large sum of money which he was expecting to collect at Le Havre. All three exchanged quick, friendly glances. Differences in social class notwithstanding, they were all conscious of belonging to a wealthy fraternity, the great freemasonry of the well-heeled who always have gold to jingle in their pockets.

The coach was moving so slowly that by ten o'clock that morning they had travelled less than ten miles. Three times the men got out to lighten the burden on the hills. They were beginning to worry again for they had hoped to stop for lunch at Tôtes and there seemed little chance now of their reaching it before nightfall. Everyone was keeping an eye out for a wayside inn when the coach sank into a snowdrift from which two hours were needed to free it once more.

Increasing hunger had begun to dampen the company's spirits. The Prussian advance, preceded as it had been by the passing of French troops on the verge of starvation, had scared away all trade and not a single eating-house or bar, however basic, was to be found anywhere en route. The gentlemen even went off hunting for food in the nearby farms but not a crumb was to be found. The wary locals had hidden away all their stores lest ravenous soldiers should rob them of all they could find.

At about one o'clock in the afternoon Loiseau declared that there was no getting away from it, he had an aching void in his stomach. Everyone had been suffering similarly for some considerable time and the craving for food, growing steadily more acute, had killed all conversation. From time to time someone would yawn, another would follow suit and each person in turn, according to character, degree of sophistication and social standing, would open his or her mouth noisily or put a polite hand over the gaping, vaporous hole.

Several times Boule de Suif leaned down and made as if to draw something out from under her petticoats. She would hesitate for a second, look over at her neighbours and then straighten up again. Every face was pale and drawn. Loiseau announced that he would give 1,000 francs for a knuckle of ham. His wife began a gesture of protest which quickly subsided. It hurt her to hear of money being wasted, even as a joke.

'I must say, I don't feel at all well,' said the Comte. 'Why on earth didn't it occur to me to bring along some provisions?' Each of the passengers was regretting precisely the same lack of foresight.

Cornudet, as it happened, had on him a flask of rum

which he offered round. It was coldly refused by all except Loiseau, who, having accepted a drop, returned the flask with thanks: 'Good stuff, that. Warms your cockles. Takes the edge off.'

The alcohol cheered him up and he suggested they do like the sailors in the shanty about the little ship where the fattest passengers were gobbled up. This oblique reference to Boule de Suif shocked his more refined companions. No one took it up and only Cornudet managed a smile. The two nuns having stopped mumbling over their rosaries now sat motionless with their hands stuffed deep into their long sleeves, eyes cast resolutely down, offering up to Heaven no doubt all the suffering now sent to test them.

At last, at three o'clock, as they were bowling along in the middle of a great plain with not a village in sight, Boule de Suif bent down quickly and drew out from under her seat a large basket covered with a white napkin. From it she took first a small china plate and a dainty little silver goblet, then an enormous terrine containing two whole chickens jointed and set in their own aspic. More goodies could be seen wrapped up in the basket; pâtés, fruit and other delicacies still. She had brought along enough provisions for three days so as not to have to depend on the unreliable cuisine of wayside inns. The necks of four bottles protruded from among the packed food. She picked up a wing of chicken and began daintily to eat it accompanied by what in Normandy is known as a Regency roll.

Every eye was fixed upon her. Then the smell of the food spread through the coach causing nostrils to distend, mouths to water and jaw muscles to contract painfully just under the ears. The ladies' contempt for this harlot turned into a fierce longing either to kill her or to throw her, with her goblet, her basket and all her provisions out into the snow. But Loiseau was devouring the terrine of chicken with his eyes.

'Well I must say,' he said. 'Madame here has had a lot more foresight than all the rest of us put together. Some people manage to think of everything.'

She turned her face towards him.

'Perhaps, Monsieur, you would care for a little something? It's awful to have had nothing to eat since morning.'

He bowed.

'I wouldn't say no, indeed. I can't hold out another minute. Wartime conditions, eh, Madame?' And glancing round at everyone, he added: 'At times like this, one is only too glad of the kindness of strangers.'

He had a newspaper which he spread on his knees so as not to get grease on his trousers and, with the point of his handy pocket-knife, speared a leg of chicken thickly coated with jelly. He tore at it with his teeth then sat munching with such obvious relish that a great sigh of distress went up from his companions.

At this, Boule de Suif in a gentle, respectful voice invited the two nuns to share her refreshments. Immediately they both accepted and, after stammering their thanks, lowered their heads and began to eat as fast as they could. Nor was Cornudet a man to reject a neighbourly gesture and the four made a sort of table by spreading newspaper over their knees.

Mouths opened and shut without pause, chewing, swallowing and gulping ravenously. Loiseau, munching solidly away in his corner urged his wife, *sotto voce*, to accept as he had. For a long time she held out but finally, after a pang of hunger pierced through to her vitals, agreed. Whereupon her husband, choosing his words carefully, asked their 'charming companion' if he might offer a small portion to Madame Loiseau. 'But of course, Monsieur,' she replied, smiling sweetly and passing him the dish. A slight difficulty arose when they opened the first bottle of claret. There was only one goblet. They passed it around with each person giving it a wipe before drinking. Only Cornudet, from gallantry it must be assumed, put it straight to his lips while it was still moist from those of his neighbour.

Surrounded by people eating and drinking, and half suffocated with the smell of food, the Comte and Comtesse de Bréville and Monsieur and Madame Carré-Lamadon were suffering the hideous torment associated with the name of Tantalus. Suddenly, the manufacturer's young wife heaved a sigh which made everyone turn and look. She was as white as the snow outside. Her eyes closed, her head fell forward and she lost consciousness.

Her distraught husband appealed for help from everyone. Nobody knew what to do except for the elder of the two nuns who, lifting her patient's head, forced Boule de Suif's goblet between her lips and made her swallow a few drops of wine. The pretty lady stirred, opened her eyes, smiled and said in a faint voice that she felt perfectly well again. To prevent a recurrence of the incident, however, the nun made her drink a whole cupful of claret, saying as she did: 'It's lack of nourishment, that's all.'

Boule de Suif, blushing with embarrassment and looking at the four travellers still without food, stammered: 'If only . . . goodness me . . . if only I might make so bold as to offer you ladies and gentlemen . . .' She broke off, fearing it might be deemed insulting.

Loiseau took up where she had left off:

'Times like this, dammit . . . all in the same boat. Help each other out. Come along ladies please, no silly nonsense now . . . For God's sake, eat up! Who knows, we may not even have a roof over our heads tonight. Way we're going . . . won't be in Tôtes before noon tomorrow . . .'

Still they hesitated. No one wanted to be the first to accept. Finally it was the Comte who settled things once and for all. Turning to the plump, shy girl with his most seigneurial air, he said: 'Madame, we are all most grateful to you.'

That was all it took. Once the Rubicon was crossed, they fell on the food like wolves. The basket was emptied and found still to contain a pâté de foie gras, a lark pâté, a piece of smoked tongue, some Crassane pears, a slab of Pont l'Evêque cheese, some petits fours and finally a jar of mixed pickled onions and gherkins since, like every other woman, Boule de Suif liked to include something raw.

They could hardly eat this girl's food without including her too in the conversation. So include her they did, albeit with a certain initial reserve which, as she turned out to have perfect manners, was soon broken down. Mesdames de Bréville and Carré-Lamadon, both ladies of great sophistication, were diplomatically gracious towards her. The Comtesse in particular, showing the kindly condescension of one whose nobility of character can be sullied by no human contact, was especially charming. Stout old Madame Loiseau, who had the soul of a sergeant-major, remained her usual surly self throughout, eating heartily and speaking little.

Naturally, they discussed the war, the terrible things done by the Prussians and the brave deeds of the heroic French. All these people running away as fast as possible from the scene of the action paid tribute to the bravery of those who stayed behind. They soon moved on to personal experiences and Boule de Suif, with the genuine passion girls have when expressing their instinctive feelings, told how she had come to leave Rouen:

'I thought to begin with that I'd stay,' she said. 'My house was well stocked-up and I thought I'd prefer to put up a few soldiers than uproot myself to goodness knows where. But when I clapped eyes on those Prussians something came over me! It just made my blood boil. I wept from shame every minute of the day. Oh, I thought, if only I was a man! I used to look at them from my window, the fat pigs, in those spiked helmets! My maid had to hold my hands down to stop me chucking furniture at them! Then some of them were sent to take up their billets with me. First one in, I went for his throat. I thought, they're no harder to strangle than any other man. I'd have finished him off, too, if they hadn't dragged me off him by the hair. After that, of course, I had to go into hiding. So, when I got the chance, I upped sticks and here I am.'

She was much praised and rose in the esteem of her fellow-travellers, none of whom had shown as much guts. Like a priest hearing one of his flock praise God, Cornudet, listening to her, smiled the benevolent and approving smile reserved for true apostles. For just as men of the cloth have a monopoly on religion, so democrats with long beards have a monopoly on patriotism. He too spoke, but in the stuffy, pompous style he had picked up from the proclamations posted daily on the walls of the city. He wound up his speech with a scathing diatribe against 'that scum of a Badinguet'.

At this, Boule de Suif, a Bonapartist as it turned out, flew into a rage. As red as a beetroot and stammering with indignation, she cried: 'I'd like to see you do any better! A right mess *you*'d have made of things! You're the very people who let him down! If France had people like you in charge we might as well all emigrate, I'm telling you!'

Although Cornudet still smiled his superior, disdainful smile, it was obvious that pretty soon the tone would be lowered, and the Comte intervened. Managing not without difficulty to calm down the furious young woman, he declared that all opinions sincerely held were worthy of respect. Nevertheless, the Comtesse and the manufacturer's wife, who harboured in their breasts the irrational hatred all respectable people have for the Republic, as well as the instinctive warmth of attachment all women feel towards strong, not to say despotic, governments, were drawn despite themselves to this dignified prostitute whose convictions so exactly mirrored their own.

The basket was now empty. Between the ten of them they had made short work of its contents and only wished it had been larger. Conversation continued for a while but languished a little after they had all finished their meal. Night was falling and with it a deepening darkness. The cold, felt all the more keenly during digestion, made Boule de Suif shiver despite her chubbiness. Seeing this, Madame de Bréville offered her the little foot-warmer which had already been refuelled several times since the morning. Boule de Suif, whose feet were freezing, accepted with alacrity. Following suit, Madame Carré-Lamadon and Madame Loiseau offered theirs to the nuns.

The coachman had lit the lanterns. They cast a vivid glare on the steaming rumps of the two horses nearest the wheels and, at each side of the road, on the snow which appeared to be unrolling under the shifting beams of light. Within the coach nothing could be made out clearly now. Suddenly, however, there was some kind of movement between Cornudet and Boule de Suif. Loiseau, his sharp eye piercing the darkness, thought he saw the long-bearded man recoil abruptly as if from some silent, well-aimed blow. Little points of light began to appear some way ahead. It was Tôtes. They had been travelling for eleven hours which, with the two hours made up by four rest periods for the horses to eat their oats, amounted to thirteen in total. They entered the town and drew up in front of the Hôtel du Commerce.

The door was opened. Then a familiar sound made all the travellers quake. It was the grating of a sword sheath against the ground. Instantly a voice cried out something in German. Although the coach had come to a complete standstill no one alighted, as if to do so were to invite massacre. The driver appeared, carrying in his hand one of the lanterns which suddenly lit up the entire interior of the carriage. Two rows of terrified faces stared out open-mouthed and wide-eyed with shock and fright.

Standing beside the driver in the full glare of the lantern was a German officer. He was a tall, fair and extremely slim young man wearing a uniform as tightly fitting as a woman's corset and, at a rakish angle on his head, a shiny pill-box of a hat which made him look like a pageboy in an English hotel. His massive moustache, with its long straight bristles tapering off on either side into a single hair so fine as to appear infinite, seemed to weigh down both the corners of his mouth and his cheeks in such a way as to make his lips droop. In a heavy Alsatian accent he invited the passengers to alight, saying curtly: 'Ladies end chentlemen get out please.'

The two nuns were the first to obey, with the meekness of holy sisters accustomed to total submission. The Comte and Comtesse appeared next, followed by the manufacturer and his wife, then by Loiseau using his better half as a shield. As soon as his feet touched the ground he said, 'Good evening Monsieur', more from prudence than politeness. The officer, with the insolence of absolute power, looked at him without replying.

Boule de Suif and Cornudet, although closest to the door, were the last to get out, grave and haughty in the presence of the enemy. The plump young girl was trying to keep some degree of self-control and remain calm. With a slightly tremulous hand the democrat tugged histrionically at his long red beard. Each wished to remain dignified, conscious that in such circumstances each person is in some respect a representative of the nation. Disgusted by her fellow citizens' easy compliance, Boule de Suif for her part was trying to muster greater self-respect than the respectable women with whom she had been travelling. Cornudet, also, feeling that it was his duty to do so, showed in his whole attitude the resistance he had begun by blocking the roads.

They entered the inn's vast kitchen where the German, having been shown the transport permit signed by the general in command, looked carefully at the travellers, checking each one against the written details. Then: 'It's good,' he said brusquely and disappeared.

They breathed once more. And since they were now hungry again, supper was ordered. It would take half an hour to prepare. While two servants busied themselves with what was obviously its preparation, they went to inspect their rooms. These were all off one long corridor, at the end of which was a glazed door marked '100'. Just as they were about to sit down at the table the innkeeper himself appeared. He was a former horse-dealer, a fat, wheezy man from whom emanated a series of bronchial whistles and gurgles. Like his father before him apparently, his name was Follenvie.

'Mademoiselle Elisabeth Rousset?' he inquired.

Boule de Suif gave a start and turned round.

'That's me, yes.'

'Mademoiselle, the Prussian officer would like a word with you immediately.'

'With me?'

'If you are Mademoiselle Elisabeth Rousset, yes.'

Disconcerted, she thought for a moment then said flatly: 'I don't care. I'm not going.'

There was a stir behind her as everyone speculated on the reason behind this summons.

The Comte approached her.

'That would be a great mistake, Madame. A refusal on your part could have disastrous consequences not only for yourself but for all your companions. You should never resist those who are stronger than you are. I'm certain there's absolutely no danger in complying with this request. It's probably just some formality that has to be cleared up.'

Everyone agreed with the Comte. She was urged and implored and lectured until in the end she was convinced. Everyone was afraid of what might happen if she followed her own fanciful impulse.

'Well as long as you know I'm only going for your sakes,' she said at last.

The Comtesse took her hand:

'And we're *so* grateful to you, really.'

She left the room and everyone waited for her to come back before sitting down at the table. Each wished it had been one of themselves who had been called rather than this violent and quick-tempered girl. They rehearsed the platitudes they would mouth should it be their turn next. In ten minutes however she was back, breathless, red in the face and choking with furious rage: 'The swine!' she stammered, 'the filthy swine!'

Everyone was longing to know, but she would reveal nothing of what had taken place.

When the Comte pressed her, she replied with great dignity, 'No! It's nothing to do with you! I don't wish to discuss it!'

They all took their places at the table around a large soup tureen from which rose the smell of cabbage. Despite the earlier setback supper was a jolly affair. The cider was good and Monsieur and Madame Loiseau, as well as the two nuns, drank it for the sake of economy. All the others ordered wine, apart from Cornudet who called for beer. He had a particular way of opening the bottle, giving the contents a good head and examining the colour in the glass which he held tilted against the light. When he drank, his large beard – which in colour took after his favourite drink – seemed to quiver with emotion. As he kept a constant, surreptitious watch on his glass, his demeanour was that of a man fulfilling the one function for which he had been put on earth. There was an undoubted affinity in his mind between the two great passions of his life: revolution and good brew. The taste of one immediately brought to mind the other.

Monsieur and Madame Follenvie were eating their supper at the far end of the table. The husband, wheezing like a broken-down locomotive, had too tight a chest to speak as well as eat, but his wife never stopped talking. She gave a comprehensive account of the Prussians' arrival, what they had done and what they had said, and cursed them first for costing her money and second because she had two sons in the army. Flattered to be in conversation with a lady of quality, she directed most of her comments to the Comtesse. Lowering her voice to broach the more delicate matters involved, she was from time to time interrupted by her husband:

'You'd better just be quiet there, Madame Follenvie.'

She took not the slightest notice and continued: 'Oh

yes, Madame, let me tell you. All they eat, this lot, is pork and potatoes. Then after that more pork and potatoes. And talk about dirty! They do their ... begging your pardon, Madame ... their business ... just anywhere. And the drilling! Hours at a time they do. Days! There they all are out in the field ... forward march, to the left ... *and* ... forward march again. If only they was working on the land or mending the roads back where they belong. But not on your life, Madame, that's soldiers for you not a scrap of good to the world. And there's us poor people having to fatten them up for what? More killing. I'm just an old woman I know ... no schooling and that, but when I see them turning themselves inside out tramping up and down from morning to night I say to myself, when you think ... how much other people are doing to discover things and then there's this lot doing as much harm as they possibly can, really ... I mean it's just horrible, isn't it, all this killing? Prussians, English, French, Polish, the lot! Say you want to get your own back on somebody who's done you harm, the law's on you, right? But when all our lads get shot down like animals, well that's fine, you get medals for that. I'm telling you, I'll never get my head round it, never.'

Cornudet raised his voice to say: 'War is barbaric when it's an attack on a peaceful neighbour, but in defence of one's country it is a sacred duty.'

The old woman bowed her head.

'In defence of the country I agree. But wouldn't it

make more sense to polish off all the kings instead? They're the ones who get all the pleasure from it.'

Cornudet's eyes flashed.

'Bravo, citizen!' he said.

Monsieur Carré-Lamadon was deep in thought. Though he had the keenest admiration for great soldiers, this captain of industry was struck by the old peasant woman's common sense. It made him think of all the wealth that could be created for the country if so many idle and therefore costly hands and so much unproductive manpower were diverted into the great industrial enterprises it would otherwise take centuries to complete.

Loiseau, getting up from his seat, went over to join the innkeeper and started whispering to him. The fat fellow coughed and spluttered and spat as he burst out laughing and his great belly heaved at his neighbour's jokes. He ordered six casks of claret to be delivered in the spring, after the Prussians had left.

As soon as supper was over, the exhausted travellers went straight up to bed.

Loiseau, however, who had been taking everything in all the while, got his wife settled into bed before putting first his ear then his eye to the keyhole so as to learn 'the secrets of the corridor' as he put it. After about an hour, hearing a slight rustle, he went quickly to look and saw Boule de Suif, looking more Rubenesque than ever in a blue cashmere dressing-gown edged with white lace. She was carrying a candle and making for the door with the number on at the end of the corridor. Yet another door, this one to the side, opened a little way, and when she returned a few minutes later Cornudet in his shirt sleeves was following her. There was a whispered conversation, then silence. It looked as though Boule de Suif was doing all she could to stop him from coming into her room. Unfortunately, to begin with Loiseau could not make out what was being said but eventually as their voices rose he managed to catch the odd phrase. Cornudet was putting on considerable pressure.

'Oh come on now, don't be silly. Why d'you make such a song and dance?'

Indignantly, she replied: 'No! Listen! There are times when you just don't do that sort of thing. Especially here. It would be disgraceful.'

It was clear that he simply did not understand. He asked her why not and at this she lost her temper. Raising her voice still further she said: 'Why not? You mean you don't *know*? When there's a *Prussian* under the same roof as you? In the next *room* maybe?'

He said no more. The patriotic propriety of this prostitute who banned sex in the presence of the enemy revived something of his own flagging sense of decency. He kissed her chastely and tiptoed quietly back to his room.

Loiseau in a state of high excitement skipped away from the keyhole, put on his nightcap and lifted the sheet beneath which lay the sturdy frame of his life's companion. Waking her with a kiss, he murmured: 'Do you love me, darling?'

After that the whole house fell silent. In a short while, however, from some indeterminate place which might have been anywhere from the cellar and the attic, rose the sound of a powerful, monotonous and regular snore; a low, prolonged rumbling with the vibrations of a boiler under pressure. Monsieur Follenvie had fallen asleep.

It had been agreed to make a start at eight and accordingly the following morning they all gathered again in the kitchen. The coach, however, its roof covered with snow stood alone in the middle of the yard with no sign of either horses or driver. They looked in vain for the latter in the stables, in the haylofts and in the coach-house. The men of the party then decided to leave the hotel and search the town for him. They found themselves in the main square with a church at one end and on either side a row of low-roofed houses in which Prussian soldiers could be seen. The first they came across was peeling potatoes. Further on, a second was scrubbing out the barbershop. Yet another, this one heavily bearded up to the eyes, was holding a crying baby on his knee and trying to rock it to sleep. Buxom peasant women whose men were 'gone for soldiers' mimed to their obedient victors what jobs needed to be done: chopping wood, ladling out soup, grinding coffee beans. One was even doing the washing for the person with whom he was billeted, who happened to be a frail old lady.

The Comte, amazed by what he saw, questioned the verger who was coming out of the presbytery.

'Oh they're all right, these lads,' said the old church mouse. 'Apparently they're not really Prussians at all. Come from further on, I'm not sure where. Every one of them's got a wife and children back home. The war's no picnic for them either, you know. I'm sure there's many a tear shed for them as well. And it'll knock them back economically, just like us. It's not so bad here for the moment. They're pretty harmless and they work just as they would at home. You see, Monsieur, we poor people, we've got to give each other a helping hand where we can. It's always the people in power that start these things.'

Cornudet, shocked by the friendly relations existing between victors and vanquished, went off, preferring to withdraw to the inn. Loiseau had to see the funny side of it: 'Repopulation, I call it.'

'Reparation, you mean,' Monsieur Carré-Lamadon gravely replied.

Still the coachman was nowhere to be seen. Eventually he was discovered in the village café sitting at the same table as the officer's orderly. The Comte hailed him: 'Weren't you told to have the horses ready by eight o'clock?'

'I was. But then I got another order.'

'What was that?'

'Not to.'

'And who gave you that order?'

'Prussian officer of course!'

'Why?'

'No idea. Go and ask him yourself. I'm told not to harness, I don't harness. Simple as that.'

'He told you himself?'

'No, monsieur. The innkeeper. On his behalf.'

'When?'

'Last night. Just when I was going to bed.'

The three men, now seriously worried, retraced their steps. They asked to see Monsieur Follenvie but were told by the maid that on account of his asthma Monsieur never got up before ten. They had strict orders not to wake him earlier unless there was a fire. They asked to see the officer but were told this was out of the question, despite the fact that his headquarters were at the inn itself. Monsieur Follenvie alone was allowed to address him on civilian matters. So they had to wait. The women went up to their rooms again and did little odds and ends of jobs to while away the time.

Cornudet settled down in the inglenook of the kitchen where a huge fire was blazing. He called for one of the little tables from the café, ordered a beer and drew out his pipe which, in local democratic circles, enjoyed almost as much prestige as he himself did, as if in serving Cornudet it too was serving its country. It was a superb meerschaum, beautifully seasoned and as black as its owner's teeth, but fragrant and gleaming. Its graceful curve fitted beautifully into his hand and rounded off the features of his face. He sat motionless, his eyes gazing now at the flames, now at the head of foam which crowned his beer. After each draught he ran his long, thin fingers through his long, greasy hair in a gesture of satisfaction and sucked through his froth-flecked moustache.

Loiseau, under the pretext of wanting to stretch his legs, went round the local retailers, taking orders for wine. The Comte and the manufacturer began to talk politics and speculated on the future of France. One was an Orleanist, the other believed in the existence of some as yet unknown saviour who would appear only when all seemed lost – another du Guesclin or another Joan of Arc, maybe? Or another Napoleon! Oh if only the Imperial Prince were not so young! Listening to them Cornudet smiled like a man from whom Fate has no secrets. The smell of his pipe pervaded the kitchen.

On the stroke of ten Monsieur Follenvie appeared. They tackled him immediately but all he did was repeat over and over the same words: 'The officer says to me, he says, Monsieur Follenvie you will give orders that the coach is not to be got ready in the morning I do not wish them to leave without my express permission, is that clear, carry on.'

They then asked to see the officer. The Comte sent in his card, to which Monsieur Carré-Lamadon had added his name and all his titles. The Prussian sent a reply saying he would hear what the two gentlemen had to say after he had had his lunch, in other words at about one o'clock.

The ladies reappeared and they all ate a little despite their anxiety. Boule de Suif looked unwell and extremely worried. They were finishing their coffee when the orderly came to fetch the gentlemen. Loiseau joined the first two, but when they attempted to rope in Cornudet so as to add more weight to the deputation he declared proudly that he had no intention of ever negotiating with the Germans. Returning to the fireside he ordered another beer.

The three men went upstairs and were admitted into the inn's best room. The officer received them, stretched out in an armchair with his feet up on the mantelpiece. He was smoking a long porcelain pipe and wearing a hideously loud dressing-gown looted no doubt from the abandoned residence of some rich man with no taste. He did not rise, did not greet nor even deign to look at them. Here was a prize example of the boorishness which is second nature to the soldier in occupation. Finally, after a while, he spoke: 'Vot is it you vant?'

The Comte acted as spokesman: 'We would like to proceed, Monsieur.'

'No.'

'And may I make so bold as to inquire the reason for this refusal?'

'Because I do not vish you to.'

'I would respectfully point out, Monsieur, that the

transport permit allowing us to travel to Dieppe is signed by your own commanding officer. I cannot see what we may have done to incur this prohibition.'

'I do not vish it. Zet is all. You may go.'

The three men bowed and withdrew. A miserable afternoon ensued. No one could understand what was behind this German's whim and the strangest ideas were entertained. Everyone remained in the kitchen debating endlessly and imagining the most unlikely scenarios. Perhaps they were going to be held hostage. But then what for? Or taken prisoner? Or held up to a hefty ransom? This thought struck terror in the hearts of all. The richest were the most terrified. They saw themselves having to hand over sacks full of gold to this arrogant soldier in order to save their skins. They racked their brains for convincing lies, strategies to conceal their wealth and pass for the poorest of the poor. Loiseau took off his watchchain and hid it in his pocket. The evening shadows fell, deepening their gloom. The lamp was lit, and since it was another two hours before dinner Madame Loiseau suggested a game of *trente-et-un*. It would take their minds off things. Everyone agreed, even Cornudet, who politely put his pipe in his pocket.

The Comte shuffled the cards and dealt. Boule de Suif got thirty-one straight away and, in the excitement of the game, the fear which was haunting their minds faded. Cornudet noticed that the Loiseau couple had a little system going which allowed them to cheat in tandem.

As they were about to sit down at the table Monsieur Follenvie reappeared.

'The Prussian officer wishes to know if Mademoiselle Elisabeth Rousset has changed her mind yet.'

Boule de Suif remained standing. At first very pale, she suddenly turned crimson, choking so much with rage that she was unable to speak. Finally she burst out: 'Tell that bastard, that sod of a Prussian, that I never will, d'you hear? Never, never, never!'

The fat innkeeper left the room. Immediately, Boule de Suif was surrounded, questioned, and implored to reveal the secret of her visit. At first she refused but very soon was carried away by her own fury.

'Want? What does he want? He wants me to sleep with him, that's what!' she cried.

Such was the general indignation that her frankness shocked no one. Cornudet slammed his glass down on the table so hard that it smashed into smithereens. There was a chorus of angry protest against the designs of this uncouth soldier, a wave of anger and as much solidarity with her as though each one had been required to share in the sacrifice demanded of her. The Comte declared with disgust that these people were behaving like barbarians. The women especially lavished intense and affectionate sympathy on Boule de Suif. The nuns, who appeared at mealtimes only, kept silent and bowed their heads. Although they all sat down to dinner after the initial furious reaction, there was little talk and much reflection.

The ladies retired early. The men, whom they left to smoke, got up a game of *écarté* to which they invited Monsieur Follenvie in the hope that some subtle questioning might reveal a way of getting round the officer's refusal. He was so absorbed in his hand, however, that he scarcely heard them, offering no reply save his oft-repeated 'Play, gentlemen, play!' So deep was his concentration on the game that he forgot to spit, a lapse which produced a few organ notes from his chest. His wheezing lungs played up and down the whole scale from deep bass to the squawking treble of the young cock's first crow. He refused to go upstairs to bed even when his wife, dropping with tiredness, came to fetch him. So she retired alone; an early bird up with the lark, as she said, she always rose at dawn while her night-owl husband was always glad to stay up with his friends till all hours. He called out to her: 'Put my egg-nog by the fire, will you?' and continued with his game.

When they realized they would get nothing out of him they decided it was time for bed themselves and retired for the night.

They rose quite early again the following morning with vague hope in their hearts and an even stronger desire to get away. The thought of yet another day in that dreary little inn filled them with horror. Alas, the horses remained in the stables and again the coachman was nowhere to be seen. For want of anything better to do they hung around the coach. Lunch was a miserable affair. There was chilliness in the general attitude towards Boule de Suif, since, having slept on the problem, her companions' views had slightly changed. Now, there was even a touch of animosity towards the prostitute. Could she not have gone on the quiet to the Prussian and given them all a lovely surprise in the morning? What could have been simpler? And who would have known? She could have saved face by telling the officer she was doing it out of pity for her companions in their plight. For her, after all, it would have been such a little thing to do. No one of course yet put these thoughts into words.

In the afternoon, since they were all bored out of their minds, the Comte suggested a walk round the village. Everyone wrapped up warmly and the little party set off, with the exception of Cornudet who preferred to stay by the fire, and the two nuns who were spending most of the day either in the church or at the priest's house. The cold which was becoming more intense every day nipped their noses and ears painfully; their feet hurt so badly that every step was torture, and when the countryside came into view it looked so appallingly bleak under its endless shroud of snow that they all turned back immediately, their spirits chilled and their hearts turned to ice. The four women walked in front while the three men followed a little way behind.

Loiseau, who had a perfect grasp of the situation, wondered aloud how long 'that whore' was going to keep them stranded in this godforsaken hole. The Comte, gallant as ever, said no woman should be asked to make such a painful sacrifice and that the answer would have to come from her herself. Monsieur Carré-Lamadon observed that if, as was likely, the French launched a counter-offensive by way of Dieppe, the place where the two armies would converge was Tôtes. This remark worried the other two.

'What if we tried to get away on foot?' said Loiseau.

The Comte shrugged his shoulders.

'In this snow? With our wives in tow? They'd be after us straight away, catch us up in ten minutes, then bring us back prisoners. At the mercy of their soldiers.'

It was all too true. Nothing more was said.

The women were talking about clothes but a certain distance was beginning to creep into their conversation. Suddenly, who should come into view at the end of the street but the officer himself. His tall figure in its wasp-waisted uniform stood out sharply against the all-encompassing snow. Knees wide apart, he was walking as soldiers do to preserve the shine on highly polished boots. He bowed as he passed the ladies and looked disdainfully at the men, who in turn maintained enough self-respect not to raise their hats, though Loiseau did make as if to do so.

Boule de Suif blushed to the roots of her hair and the three married ladies felt deeply humiliated at being seen by an officer in the company of the prostitute treated by him in such a cavalier way. They began to talk about him, commenting on his looks and general appearance. Madame Carré-Lamadon, who had known a great many officers in her time and considered herself a connoisseur, found him not bad at all. A pity he wasn't French – he'd have made a very handsome hussar and all the women would have fallen for him.

Back at the inn, they no longer knew what to do with themselves. Harsh words were exchanged over mere trifles. Dinner was a brief and silent occasion and everyone went up to bed hoping to kill time by sleeping.

They came down the next morning with tired faces and frayed tempers. The men hardly spoke to Boule de Suif. A church bell began to ring. It was for a christening. The plump young woman had a child, it turned out, who was being looked after by a peasant family in Yvetot. From one year's end to the next, she neither saw it nor gave it a thought. But the thought of this one now filled her heart with a sudden overwhelming feeling of love for her own. She decided she simply had to attend the ceremony.

No sooner had she left than they all looked at each other and drew together their chairs. It was high time they came to some sort of a decision. Loiseau had an idea. What about suggesting the officer keep Boule de Suif alone and allow the others to go? Monsieur Follenvie once more agreed to act as go-between but returned almost immediately. The German, wise in the ways of the world, had shown him the door. Everyone must remain until his wishes were carried out.

At this, Madame Loiseau's vulgar instincts broke out.

'We're surely not going to sit here for the rest of our days, are we? It's that slut's job to do it with any man. She's got no right to pick and choose. I mean, I ask you! She takes any man in the whole of Rouen, even coachmen! Yes, Madame, even the Prefect's coachman! I happen to know because he buys his wine from us. And now, when it comes to getting us out of this pickle, that tart starts to get sniffy! As a matter of fact, I think the officer's behaved pretty well. Who knows how long he's been without? And there's the three of us he'd probably much prefer really. But there you are, he makes do with a common prostitute. He respects married women. Just think! He's in charge. He'd only have to give his soldiers the word and have us taken by force!'

The two other women gave a little shudder. Madame Carré-Lamadon's eyes flashed and her face paled as if already in the clutches of the officer. The men, who had been conferring privately, returned to the ladies. Loiseau, beside himself with anger, wanted the wretched girl bound hand and foot and handed over to the officer. But the Comte, the product of three generations of ambassadors, and himself the soul of diplomacy, advocated a subtler approach.

'We must make her see the sense of it herself,' he said.

They began to hatch a plot. The women huddled closer together, voices were lowered, and in the general discussion which ensued each had something to contribute. The

129

ladies in particular found delicate turns of phrase, charming euphemisms to convey the crudest ideas. So carefully worded were their proposals that a stranger to the whole business would never guess what exactly it was they were suggesting. The veneer of modesty in every worldly woman is skin deep only, and they therefore relished the naughtiness of it all, savouring every salacious detail like greedy chefs preparing with loving care the supper others are to eat.

The whole thing was so richly amusing that the mood of the party eventually lifted. The Comte made a few slightly risqué quips that were so cleverly turned you had to smile. Loiseau in turn added some coarser ones to which no one really objected. The general consensus, somewhat crudely expressed by his wife, was that since it's a prostitute's job to take on all and sundry, this one had no more right to refuse him than to debar any other man. Dear little Madame Carré-Lamadon went so far as to say that were she in Boule de Suif's place she would find the officer rather more acceptable than most. Detailed plans were made for the siege ahead. Each was allotted a part in the action and given an argument to use or a particular manoeuvre to deploy. A plan of attack was laid, complete with stratagems which included surprise assaults to force this human citadel to yield publicly to the authority of the enemy. Cornudet, however, kept aloof and refused to have anything at all to do with it.

So deeply were they absorbed that no one heard Boule

de Suif return. The Comte's whispered 'shush' made everyone look up. There she was. Everyone stopped talking at once and, at first, a feeling of embarrassment prevented them from speaking to her. At last, the Comtesse, more practised than the others in the art of salon politics, asked: 'And did you enjoy the christening?'

The plump young woman, still moved by the ceremony, gave them all the details of it, describing people's faces, their expressions, their demeanour and even the church itself, adding: 'Does you good, doesn't it, to say a little prayer every once in a while?'

Until it was time for lunch the ladies contented themselves with being agreeable to her, thereby lulling her into a false sense of security which might make her more amenable to their advice later on. As soon as they sat down to eat, however, the first approaches were made. There was an initially general discussion on the subject of self-sacrifice. Historical examples were quoted: Judith and Holophernes; then, irrelevantly, Lucretia and Sextus; and Cleopatra, who took all her enemy generals into her bed and reduced them to slavish obedience to her will. This was followed by a wholly fictitious tale cobbled together from the imagination of these moneyed ignoramuses in which the women of ancient Rome travelled to Capua where they lulled to sleep in their arms not only Hannibal but all his lieutenants, as well as his phalanxes of mercenaries. They cited examples of all sorts of women who had halted invading hordes in their tracks by turning their own bodies into a battlefield, and won over with their heroic caresses hideous and hated oppressors, thereby sacrificing their chastity on the altar of devotion and revenge.

There was even a veiled reference to the English aristocrat who had herself injected with a fatal and contagious disease so as to transmit it to Bonaparte, who was miraculously saved by a last-minute indisposition that prevented his meeting both the lady and his own death. All these stories were told in a sober, matter-of-fact manner with occasional bursts of enthusiasm calculated to inspire emulation. To hear them talk, one might have thought that a woman's sole duty on earth was the perpetual sacrifice of her person as she became the bawd of all barrack-room boys.

The two nuns, deep in meditation throughout, appeared to hear nothing. Boule de Suif remained silent. All afternoon they left her to her own thoughts. However, instead of addressing her as 'Madame' as had hitherto been their practice, without knowing why they now used mere 'Mademoiselle' as if wishing to shift her down from the heights of respectability she had scaled and make her feel the shamefulness of her position.

As soon as soup was served, Monsieur Follenvie appeared, repeating the previous day's formula: 'The Prussian officer wishes to know whether Mademoiselle Elisabeth Rousset has still not changed her mind.'

Boule de Suif replied curtly: 'No, monsieur.'

Over dinner, the coalition weakened. Loiseau made

three somewhat unfortunate remarks. Everyone was racking their brains to think of yet more role-models, when the Comtesse, possibly without premeditation beyond a vague desire to give a little nod to religion, questioned the elder of the nuns on the great events in the lives of the saints. Apparently many had committed what we would call crimes, but which the Church had forgiven since they were done for the glory of God or out of neighbourly love. This was a powerful argument and the Comtesse made the most of it. Then, whether by a tacit understanding or a veiled complicity in which men and women of the cloth excel, or whether through blissful ignorance and fortuitous stupidity, the old nun contributed hugely to the conspiracy. While they had considered her timid, she now showed herself bold, forceful and articulate. Not for her the groping hesitancies of casuistry in grasping the truth. Her doctrine was as solid as a bar of iron, her faith equally unshakeable and her conscience unclouded by a single doubt. Abraham's sacrifice of his son Isaac seemed to her the most natural phenomenon in the world. She would have dispatched unhesitatingly both mother and father if the order had come from above. In her view, nothing could fail to please God if it stemmed from laudable intentions. The Comtesse, taking advantage of the sacred authority vested in her unsuspected ally, made her construct an edifying paraphrase of the precept that the end justifies the means. She pressed her: 'So . . . Sister . . . you mean . . . all means are acceptable to God and that he pardons any action whose motive is pure?'

'Who could doubt it, Madame? A reprehensible action in itself is often meritorious by virtue of the idea which inspires it.'

And so they went on, interpreting the will of God, predicting his decisions and making him allegedly interested in things that were hardly any of his concern. All this was couched in allusive, veiled and discreet language. Yet every word emanating from under the holy wimple took its toll on the indignant resistance of the prostitute. Then the conversation took a different turn as our lady of the rosary talked about the different houses of her order, about her Mother Superior, about herself and her sweet companion, dear Sister Nicéphore. They were being sent to Le Havre to nurse the hundreds of soldiers there suffering from smallpox. She described these poor wretches and their disease in detail. To think that while they were being held up on the whim of this Prussian, so many French lives which could otherwise be saved were going to be lost! Military nursing was her field; she had been out in the Crimea, in Italy and in Austria, and as she recounted all the campaigns she had experienced, she was revealed as a real banner-carrying Sister Hannah bearing the wounded off the field and quelling with a single glance the toughest of undisciplined other ranks. She was a seasoned old warhorse whose ravaged, pockmarked face symbolized perfectly the devastation of war.

After her excellent contribution, there was no need for anyone to add a single word. As soon as the meal was over, everyone went straight up to their rooms and did not appear till late the following morning. There followed a quiet lunch during which the seed planted the previous day was given time to germinate and bear fruit.

In the afternoon, the Comtesse suggested a walk. As planned, the Comte offered his arm to Boule de Suif and lingered with her a little way behind the others. He spoke to her in the familiar, paternal, slightly patronizing way certain mature men of the world use with women of her sort, calling her 'my child' and talking down to her from the heights of his well-established respectability and infinitely superior social rank.

'So . . . you would prefer to make us languish here, exposed like yourself to all the outrages which would ensue if the Prussians were to suffer a reversal, rather than perform another one of the many services necessary to your way of life?'

Boule de Suif made no reply. He tried all sorts of means on her, including gentle persuasion and an appeal to both her reason and her finer feelings in turn. He maintained the dignity required of his social position, while simultaneously playing the flattering and gallant ladies' man when necessary. He stressed what a huge favour she would be doing them all, and how enormously grateful they would all be. Then suddenly, addressing her as an intimate, he said: 'And I'll tell you something, my dear, he'll be able to brag he's had a prettier girl than any back where he comes from!'

Boule de Suif made no response and moved to join the rest of the party.

Immediately upon her return, she went up to her room and did not reappear. The suspense mounted. What was she going to do? How awful if she continued to hold out! The hour struck for dinner. They waited for her in vain. Then Monsieur Follenvie came in, announcing that Mademoiselle Rousset was indisposed and that they should begin without her. Everyone pricked up their ears. The Comte went over to the innkeeper and whispered: 'Everything going all right then?'

'Yes.'

Out of propriety he conveyed none of this verbally to his companions but gave them a very slight nod. At this a huge sigh of relief went up and every face brightened. Loiseau cried: 'Well I'll be . . . ! Champagne! On me! If there *is* any in this establishment.'

To his wife's obvious dismay the landlord returned with four bottles. Suddenly everyone became very noisy and voluble and the party was full of ribald merriment. The Comte appeared to notice for the first time Madame Carré-Lamadon's charms. The manufacturer in turn began paying flattering compliments to the Comtesse. The conversation became gay and lively, not to say racy.

Suddenly Loiseau with a concerned expression on his face raised his arms and cried: 'Quiet!'

Surprised and even a little scared again, everyone stopped talking. Cocking his ear and holding up his hands for silence, he raised his eyes ceilingwards, listened again then continued in a normal voice: 'Nothing to worry about. Everything's fine.'

A quarter of an hour later he went through the same performance, repeating it several times throughout the evening. From time to time he would hold an imaginary conversation with someone on the floor above, dredging up every lewd innuendo and double entendre with which his dirty little mind was stocked. At times he would put on a pained expression and breathe, 'Oh the poor girl!' Or again, muttering angrily between clenched teeth, 'Oh you swine of a Prussian, you!' Often, when the conversation had moved on he would repeat in a voice quivering with emotion: 'Stop it will you! That's enough!' adding, as if to himself, 'Let's hope she lives to tell us the tale! That he's not the death of her, the bastard!'

Though the jokes were in the most deplorable taste, everyone, far from being shocked, was in fits of laughter. Indignation, like everything else is the product of environment and the atmosphere gradually created around them was by now frankly bawdy. By dessert, even the women were making risqué little remarks. Eyes were sparkling and much wine had been drunk. The Comte, who even in his cups maintained a façade of great seriousness, made a much enjoyed comparison between their present situation and that of shipwrecked sailors at the

Pole when winter ends and an escape route to the south opens up.

Loiseau, by now well away, stood up with a glass of champagne in his hand, crying, 'I drink to our deliverance!' Everyone rose to their feet and applauded him. Even the two nuns, urged by the ladies, agreed to take the tiniest sip of the sparkling wine never tasted by them before. They concluded it was just like fizzy lemonade, only more delicate of course. Loiseau caught the general mood when he said, 'Pity there isn't a piano. We could have had a bit of a prance.'

Cornudet throughout had not uttered a single word nor made a single gesture. On the contrary, he appeared plunged in serious thought, tugging angrily at his beard from time to time as if to lengthen it still further. Finally, around midnight just as the party was breaking up, Loiseau staggered over to him, dug him in the ribs and slurred: 'Barrel of laughs you are, tonight, I must say. S'madder with you?'

Cornudet simply raised his head sharply, threw a fierce glare round the entire company and said, 'The way you've all behaved tonight's disgraceful!'

He got up and, reaching the door, added: 'Absolutely disgraceful!'

At first this cast something of a pall. Loiseau, a little stunned, stood gawping and then, recovering his wits, he doubled up with laughter.

'Sour grapes, my friend! That's what it is . . . sour grapes!'

Since no one got the joke he explained the 'secrets of the corridor'. At this, there was a great burst of renewed mirth. The ladies were in hysterics. The Comte and Madame Carré-Lamadon laughed till they cried. They could not believe it.

'You mean . . . ? You're sure . . . ? He wanted to . . . ?'

'I tell you I *saw* him!'

'And she wouldn't . . .'

'Because the Prussian was in the next room.'

'Never!'

'I swear to God.'

The Comte was choking with laughter. The industrialist was holding his sides. Loiseau went on: 'So you see why he doesn't see the funny side of it tonight! Not funny at all, *oh* no!'

And they were off again, coughing and choking and making themselves sick with laughter. At this point the party split up. Madame Loiseau commented in her waspish way, as she and her husband were getting into bed, that 'that little minx' Madame Carré-Lamadon had had a touch of the green-eyed monster in her eyes all evening. 'Some women'll go for anything in uniform. They don't give a hoot what sort. French, Prussian, you name it. Honest to God, it makes you weep!'

All night long from the darkness of the corridor all

sorts of soft, barely audible sounds could be heard – faint rustles and creaks and the patter of bare feet on boards. From the narrow strips of light showing under the door-ways it was clear that no one got to sleep until very late. Champagne is like that, it has the effect of a stimulant, apparently.

The following day, the winter sun shone brightly on the dazzling snow. Hitched up at last, the coach stood waiting at the front door while an army of white pigeons with black-centred pink eyes preened themselves as they strutted importantly between the legs of the six horses and pecked for food in the steaming dung.

The coachman, wrapped up in his sheepskin on the box, was puffing at his pipe as the ecstatic travellers all hurriedly packed in provisions for the remainder of the journey. Only Boule de Suif was missing. At last she appeared. She looked anxious and shamefaced. As she timidly approached her companions they turned, as one, away from her as if she were invisible. The Comte offered a dignified arm to his wife and led her away from possibly degrading contact. The plump young woman, shocked, stopped in her tracks. Then, summoning all her courage, she went up to the manufacturer's wife and mur-mured politely: 'Good morning, Madame.'

The other woman in reply gave the curtest of contemp-tuous nods, accompanied by a glare of outraged virtue. Affecting to be very busy, everyone kept their distance as though she were carrying some infection in her skirts.

Rushing to the coach they left her to arrive last and alone to take the seat she had previously occupied during the first part of the journey. They appeared neither to see nor to recognize her. Madame Loiseau, however, looking indignantly over in her direction, muttered to her husband: 'Thank goodness I'm not sitting next to *her*.'

The heavy carriage jerked into motion and they set off once more on their journey. At first no one spoke. Boule de Suif dared not look up. She felt simultaneously angry with her neighbours, humiliated by having given in to them, and defiled by the caresses of the Prussian into whose arms they had so hypocritically thrown her.

The Comtesse, however, turning towards Madame Carré-Lamadon, soon broke the awkward silence.

'I believe you know Madame d'Etrelles?'

'Oh yes, she's a great friend of mine.'

'What a delightful woman!'

'Charming. Very special indeed. Well-educated too and an artist to the tips of her fingers. She has a wonderful voice and she draws like a dream, did you know?'

The manufacturer was talking to the Comte and above the rattle of the window panes the occasional word or phrase could be heard: 'Dividends . . . maturity date . . . option . . . mature . . .'

Loiseau who had stolen the ancient pack of cards belonging to the inn and greasy with five years' contact with sticky table-tops, embarked on a game of bezique with his wife.

The two nuns, taking up the long rosaries that hung from their belts, made a simultaneous sign of the cross. Suddenly their lips began to move at an ever-increasing speed as if competing in some *salve regina* steeplechase. From time to time they would kiss a medal, cross themselves again, then once more take up the mumbling at a rate of knots. Cornudet sat motionless, lost in thought. After three hours' travelling Loiseau gathered up his cards. 'Time to eat,' he said.

At this his wife reached for a packet tied up with string from which she extracted a joint of cold veal. She cut it into neat, thin slices and the two began to tuck in.

'Perhaps we should follow your example,' said the Comtesse.

A chorus of approval rose and she set about unpacking the provisions which had been prepared for the two couples. In one of those long, oval vessels with a china hare for a lid indicating that within there lay a *lièvre en paté*, a succulent piece of charcuterie in which the hare's dark flesh mixed together with other finely chopped meats was streaked with white rivulets of bacon fat. There was also a fine slab of Gruyère, wrapped in newspaper and now carrying the words 'NEWS IN BRIEF' on its satiny surface. The two nuns unwrapped a hunk of garlicky *saucisson* and Cornudet, plunging his hands into the gigantic patch pockets of his greatcoat, brought out from one of them four hard-boiled eggs, and from the other the crusty end of a loaf. The shells of the eggs he threw into the straw at his feet, and as he munched each in turn a constellation of bright yellow flecks was scattered into the dark firmament of his beard.

When she rose that morning Boule de Suif had been in such haste and trepidation that she had had no time to think of anything. Choking with rage, she now looked on as around her all these people carried on calmly eating. A wave of anger surged over her and she opened her mouth to release the torrent of abuse she felt rising within her. It was so deep, however, that she was unable to utter a word. No one looked at her. No one gave her a thought. She felt overwhelmed by the contempt of these respectable swine who, having used her as a scapegoat, now rejected her as something unclean. She thought then about her great big basket full of the goodies they had greedily devoured – her two glistening chickens in aspic, her pears and her four bottles of claret. Suddenly, like a piece of string stretched to breaking-point, her anger collapsed and left her on the verge of tears. She tried desperately to control her feelings, bracing herself and swallowing back her sobs like a child. The tears welled up regardless, glistening at the tips of her eyelids. Soon two great drops, brimming over, fell and rolled slowly down her cheeks. Others followed, flowing faster. Like drops of water trickling from a rock they fell in steady succession on to the rounded curve of her bosom. She sat erect, staring directly ahead with a set expression. She hoped no one would notice.

The Comtesse, however, did, and nudged her husband. He shrugged his shoulders as if to say, 'Well? It's nothing to do with me.' Madame Loiseau gave a quiet snigger of triumph and muttered, 'She's crying from shame, that's all.' The two nuns, having rewrapped the remainder of their *saucisson*, returned to their prayers.

Then Cornudet still digesting his eggs stretched out his long legs under the seat opposite, leaned back, folded his arms and smiled. He had just thought of a great joke: softly, he began to whistle the *Marseillaise*.

Across every face a shadow fell. The song of the Republic was obviously not a favourite of his neighbours. They shifted about uncomfortably in their seats and looked ready to howl like dogs at a barrel-organ. Well aware of its effect he continued with the song regardless. From time to time he even mouthed some of the words:

> *Amour sacré de la patrie,*
> *Conduis, soutiens, nos bras vengeurs,*
> *Liberté, liberté chérie,*
> *Combats avec tes défenseurs!*

> (O sacred love of Fatherland,
> Guide and support our venging hands,
> Dear freedom, dearest Liberty,
> Staunch guardians with us ever be!)

They were gathering speed since the snow was harder now. All the way to Dieppe, throughout the long, tedious hours of the journey along the bumpy roads, as twilight turned to night inside the coach, he kept up his monotonous, vengeful whistling, dinning into his weary and exasperated companions every word and every note.

Boule de Suif wept on, and, from time to time, in the pause between verses, a sob she was helpless to stifle escaped into the darkness.

Dorothy Parker · *Big Blonde* · 9780241609934

Edgar Allan Poe · *The Masque of the Red Death* · 9780241573754

Alexander Pushkin · *The Queen of Spades* · 9780241573761

Rainer Maria Rilke · *Letters to a Young Poet* · 9780241620038

Saki · *Reginald's Christmas Revel* . 9780241597026

Arthur Schnitzler · *Dream Story* · 9780241620229

John Steinbeck · *Of Mice and Men* · 9780241620236

Leo Tolstoy · *The Cossacks* · 9780241573778

Yuko Tsushima · *Territory of Light* · 9780241620243

Sylvia Townsend Warner · *Lolly Willowes* · 9780241573785

Oscar Wilde · *The Star-Child* · 9780241597033

Virginia Woolf · *Street Haunting* · 9780241597040

In Preparation

Jorge Luis Borges · *The Library of Babel* · 9780241630860

Albert Camus · *The Fall* · 9780241630778

Kate Chopin · *The Awakening* · 9780241630785

F. Scott Fitzgerald · *Babylon Revisited* · 9780241630839

Clarice Lispector · *The Imitation of the Rose* · 9780241630846

Yukio Mishima · *Death in Midsummer* · 9780241630853

Vladimir Nabokov · *Nabokov's Dozen* · 9780241630884

Françoise Sagan · *Bonjour Tristesse* · 9780241630891

Sam Selvon · *Calypso in London* · 9780241630877

Georges Simenon · *My Friend Maigret* · 9780241630792

Edith Wharton · *Summer* · 9780241630815

Stefan Zweig · *Chess* · 9780241630822